MAIL ORDER MISFIT

Mail Order Mix-Up Series Book 1

JENNA BRANDT

COPYRIGHT

PRAISE FOR JENNA BRANDT

I'm always excited when I see a new book by Jenna Brandt. This very talented author can create an amazing storyline without missing a beat!

— LORI DYKES, AMAZON
CUSTOMER

Jenna Brandt is, in my estimation, the most gifted author of Christian fiction in this generation!

— PAULA ROSE MICHELSON,
CHRISTIAN ROMANCE AUTHOR

Jenna Brandt writes from the heart and you can feel it in every page turned.

— SANDRA SEWELL WHITE,
LONGTIME READER

Jenna Brandt does a good job of pulling you in quickly and creating characters that you care about.

I love this author - She always writes intriguing and amazing stories. She can write in any time period and owns it.

Thank you Jenna Brandt for good wholesome novels that focus on Christian values.

For more information about Jenna Brandt, signup for her Newsletter or visit her on any of her social media platforms:

www.JennaBrandt.com

www.facebook.com/JennaBrandtAuthor

Jenna Brandt's Reader Group

www.instagram.com/jennabrandtauthor

To all those who love to read.
Let's enjoy a story together.

CHAPTER ONE

Dakota Territory, 1885

The sprawling Great Plains of North America continued to pass by through the window of the train. The steep, flat-topped hills, better known as buttes, dominated the landscape of the James River Valley. Soon Cara McGregor would be arriving in the town of Mitchell, where her whole life would change forever.

She read the letter from her future husband another time, still trying to accept that she was traveling out West to meet the man willing to marry her. James Cassidy sounded like a good man, a man she could find contentment with, since love wasn't in the cards for her.

Considering her reputation back in her hometown of Hull, Massachusetts, she was glad the man hadn't requested to know more about her family situation. It wasn't good. She left behind a place filled with Irish folk from the Old Country, whom by the end of her time in Hull, treated her like a leper because of what happened with her parents.

She wished she could have gone back to that day and been at the house when her mother was killed. If she had seen what happened instead of being off with her beau, the townspeople wouldn't have blamed her father and hung him two months later for the crime.

She not only lost her parents that day, but her beau along with any future prospects of marriage, since everyone in town viewed her as the spawn of the devil himself. It was as if everyone forgot what a good man her father had been; looking out for his neighbors, helping at the church, and taking care of his family.

The little money her parents had saved ran out by the end of the second month. She couldn't get a job for the same reasons as she couldn't land a husband. All that was left was to start over somewhere else, and she remembered that Josephine Little had found a groom out West through a mail-order advertisement. With nothing left to lose, Cara found herself scouring The Matrimonial Times.

She could still remember the words of Mr. Cassidy's advert in the newspaper. *Needed, Wife. South Dakota widower seeks a kind, faithful woman to run his household on his farm, to support his work, and rear his three children. Due to conditions in the rural area, only a strong, diligent woman of fortitude and grit need reply.*

Cara should have dismissed it out of hand, considering she had no business doing any of the work he required, but something about the unspoken plea in the request pulled at Cara's heart. She needed a new life, and she could help this man while gaining one. What could it hurt to answer?

Two letters and a month later, she was headed out West with only two bags, and her gumption to make the marriage work. She hoped she was able to live up to her new family's expectations, though she had little experience in running a household or mothering children. Her best example was her own mother, who had been loving, helpful, and always there for her. She hoped to provide the same care for her new wards. She was resolved to be the best match for Mr. Cassidy, rather than just a misfit for his family.

Deciding she could use some air, Cara stood from her seat in the car she shared with a family and a widow traveling to Oregon. She slipped the letter into her pocket, and made her way towards the back of the train. She was about to exit through the back door, when a man came up and blocked her path.

"Why aren't you the prettiest little thing I've ever seen?" the man said with a wag of his eyebrows. He reached out and grabbed a strand of her hair, rubbing it between his fingers and thumb. "I've always had an inkling for redheads."

She shrank back, not liking how close the man was, or the fact he felt justified enough to touch her. "I'll just be going now," she said, trying to push past him to return from the way she came.

Putting out his arm to block her path, he observed, "I thought you were headed to the back of the train? No one's around by the way, so we have the whole section to ourselves."

"I've changed my mind," Cara declared, raising her chin in defiance, while trying to muster her bravest face.

"You needn't hurry off on my account," the

man said, leaning in towards her until she could smell the repugnant odor of liquor on his breath. "I've got all the time in the world."

"Well, I don't," she stated tartly. "I have people waiting for me back in my car."

"I don't think so, missy. I've been watching you for a while, and you're traveling alone. Ain't no one worrying about your whereabouts. I doubt anyone would care what happens to you," he snarled, pushing his body against hers as his hand started to roam all over her body.

"Don't touch me," she screamed, squirming against him in anger. "Get your hands off me."

"Did I tell you, that's my favorite part about redheads? Nothin' more appealin' than a redhead's temper. I love it when they get all feisty," he said with a leering grin of pleasure.

Cara froze, realizing that this man wanted her to fight him. It made him excited, and that was the last thing she wanted to encourage.

As she stood perfectly still, she slowly moved her hand down her side. She finally reached the strap inside the hidden insert of her pocket where she carried a small knife. She whipped it out as fast she could, pushing it towards the man's chest.

"If you don't get away from me right now, I'm going to make you a new hole."

The man's eyes grew wide in shock for a few moments before he narrowed them in anger. "Are you sure you can use that knife, missy? I'm bettin' you've never stabbed a man. It's messy, with a lot of blood." He reached out and tried to grab the knife from her, but she dodged his reach.

"It's better than the alternative," she shouted. "I won't have you ruin me."

"Can't ruin something that's already tarnished," he barked out. "You wouldn't be traveling all alone if you were a good woman."

The man lunged at her again. This time his hand made contact with hers, causing them to wrestle for control of the knife. She was about to lose her grip on the hilt when a group of miners entered the car.

"What's going on here?" one of the men shouted with a look of shock on his face.

Her attacker looked fearful for the briefest of moments before he accused, "This thief tried to rob me. I was coming out back to get some air, when she tried to pickpocket me. When I confronted her, she pulled a knife on me."

"That's not what happened," Cara protested. "I

was the one coming out back to get air when he accosted me. He had vile intentions, so I had to pull my knife to protect myself."

"What respectable woman would need to carry a knife around?" the attacker countered. "Only someone who has a devious nature."

"I'm traveling alone, so I brought one of my father's knives along for protection," Cara said, trying to explain away how bad the situation looked on her part.

She could tell from the miners' looks, they doubted her story, and her explanation sounded ridiculous even to her own ears.

"Perhaps one of us should go get the conductor to sort this matter out," a second man suggested.

"I think that's a good idea. I would like to tell him all about how this thief behaved," her attacker stated with confidence. "She'll hang for trying to kill me. I'll make sure of it."

A shiver crawled up Cara's back as she realized this man wanted to make her pay for not getting his way with her. If she didn't escape right now, she was going to end up dangling from a hangman's noose. Glancing out the window, she realized they were slowing down as they approached a set of curves on the rail line. If she jumped off the train now, she'd only suffer a few bumps and bruises, a much better alternative.

Without another thought, Cara turned and rushed towards the door. She swung it open, and flung herself through it. For just a split second, she paused as she came to the edge of the iron railing. Knowing she had no choice, she climbed over and threw herself from the side.

The left side of her body met the ground with a hard thud, right before she started rolling down the small hill. She could feel the dirt and rocks tearing at her flesh; however, she made herself ignore the pain and focus on getting as far away from the train as possible. If she got arrested, it would end badly for her. No one at home would vouch for her, considering her family's history, and some would even say that it made sense that she turned out just like her father. She would be assumed guilty simply because of her family's past.

The shouts of the men from the train echoed around Cara as she rushed along the bank of the James River. Slowly, they faded as she slipped away into her surroundings, praying she would find some way to survive out in the frontier wilderness.

———

As James Cassidy got ready to head into town, he continued to remind himself he was doing the right thing, at least for his children, if not for himself. He would have been content to remain unmarried forever after the death of his first wife. His children, however, needed a mother even though Susan, his eldest child, would argue differently.

Over the past year, he'd been doing a horrible job of balancing taking care of his farm and children, prompting him to place an advert in The Matrimonial Times.

He had thought it a silly notion at first, but with so few women in the South Dakota frontier, he had no means of finding another wife. Desperate times called for desperate measures, and James had never been so desperate as he was right now. He just hoped that Cara McGregor would be what she advertised in her introductory letter.

She sounded sensible and capable, though maybe a little naïve about what it was going to take to do the work he would need. Her straightforwardness in stating her limitations, rather than trying to cover them up or avoid discussing them, made him sure she would be an asset to his home and family. This prompted him to send a letter in return offering travel money and marriage once she arrived in Mitchell.

Thomas, his youngest and only boy, came bursting into James' bedroom, carrying a toad in his hands. "Look what I found outside in the stream, Pa. I couldn't find Becky to scare—she must be hiding—so I scared Susan with it instead. She stormed inside the house and threw herself on the sofa."

James stood to his feet and crossed his arms, giving his son an irritated look. Great, all he needed was Susan to be out of sorts right before he went into town. She needed to have her wits about her while he was gone, considering she had to watch after both Thomas, and his middle child, Becky. He didn't want any trouble while he was gone.

"You shouldn't have done that, Thomas. You know how sensitive Susan is lately; you shouldn't go picking on her all the time."

"But it's funny to see her face turn all red like a tomato. Sometimes I think she's going to explode, she gets so mad," Thomas said with a lopsided grin.

James wanted to stay angry at his son, but part of him agreed. Susan tended to get vexed over almost everything lately, but he had to remind himself a lot had been thrust on her at the tender age of twelve. She had to take on the job of mothering her siblings while still grieving the loss of her ma, not to mention the cooking and taking care of the home. It wasn't fair to ask so much of any child, but soon he would be able to change all of that once Cara was living with them. Susan could go back to being a kid.

James bent down to look into the blue eyes of his son, the same as his mother's. "I understand that you think it's funny, but you need to give an extra measure of kindness to your sisters right now. It's been hard on all of us without your ma around."

The boy nodded, a sadness entering his eyes only for a moment before he quickly shook his head. "But today we get a new Ma, so that means I can go back to teasing my sisters."

"No, that's not what that means," James said, ruffling the blond hair on his son's head. "It just means we all might find a way to get back to a routine around here."

James exited his bedroom with Thomas close on his heels. As they entered the living area of the small ranch home, he found Susan still sniffling on the sofa. He made his way over to his eldest daughter and sat down beside her. Awkwardly, he patted her on the back, not quite sure if he was doing it right. Laura had been the one to tend to the matters with the children.

"Are you all right, Susan?" James inquired with concern.

"No, I'm not all right," Susan shrieked out as she flipped over, causing her long blonde hair to fan out across the sofa. "Thomas nearly caused my heart to stop beating. I thought I was going to die just like Ma did, I swear it."

"You know that wouldn't happen, Susan. Please don't exaggerate," James requested.

Crossing her arms over her chest, she narrowed her brown eyes in anger as she spat out, "Of course you take his side, like always. I do everything around here, but since he's the baby, he gets away with every rotten thing he does to me and Becky."

"That's not true, Susan. I already talked with Thomas and told him not to tease either of you anymore."

"That's it? You talked to him? What if I get a wart from that toad touching me? Then no boy will ever love me," she shrieked out again as fresh tears fell down her cheeks. She turned her face back into the pillow, blocking out the fresh sobs that were causing her whole body to shake.

James wasn't equipped to deal with this sort of

outburst, and it had been happening more and more all the time. Unable to console his daughter, he stood up and made his way to the front door.

"Where's Becky?" he asked in a general way, hoping she was hiding somewhere in the house so he didn't have to go outside to hunt for her before he left for town.

"I already told you, she's hiding from me," Thomas proclaimed.

"You don't have to hide anymore, Becky. Your pa is right here," James said in a coaxing voice.

After several seconds passed, a small brown-haired girl, the only one of his children to take after his side of the family, emerged from out of one of the kitchen cabinets.

"Is it really safe to come out?" Becky probed, giving a skeptical look at her brother.

"Of course, it is," James promised. "Thomas is going to be on his best behavior while I'm in town picking up Miss Cara."

"You mean our new ma," Thomas corrected.

Hearing Thomas so quickly replace their mother made James want to scream. No one would ever be their new ma, but he knew it wasn't the seven year old's fault. He didn't know any better.

"Well, I don't think we should rightly call her

that until she's had some time to adjust to all of us," James stated instead. "We need to give her time to become familiar with our home."

"And then we can start calling her Ma," Thomas stated firmly.

"She's never going to be our ma," declared Susan, rolling her face from the pillow just long enough to shout her refusal. "Never, never!"

Not knowing what to do, James decided to leave anyway, hoping for the best while he was gone. "I have to go children, but I'll be home in a couple of hours. Please be good and don't get into any trouble, or there will be severe consequences," he warned, though he didn't even know what their punishment would be, since again, Laura had doled them out.

None of the children responded, not giving any measure of peace to James as he left his home.

As he drove his wagon towards town, he wondered if Cara would be as pretty as her picture. He'd heard stories of women switching their photographs in order to have a better chance of landing a husband. He hoped that wasn't the case. The woman in the picture was quite attractive. He wasn't sure it was fair of him to care about her looks, considering his biggest priority was to find a helpmate, not a romantic interest. He had no delusions about finding love twice in his life. He had firmly set that notion aside; however, having an attractive woman sitting across the dinner table would be an added bonus to anything else Cara McGregor had to offer.

An hour later, he arrived at the train depot in Mitchell. He climbed down from his wagon, secured his horse, and made his way to the platform.

After some time passed, he checked his pocket watch and noted the train was late. Not an unusual occurrence around these parts, but every minute that passed made James worry about his children at home. He didn't want to seem anxious when Cara arrived. He sent up a silent prayer, asking God to calm his nerves, and to protect everything at home while he was away.

Gratitude filled his heart when the train finally arrived. He wasn't sure how much longer he could've waited to meet his future wife.

She wasn't with the first set of people off the train, but perhaps she was gathering her bags. He waited, and waited, but as the passengers dwindled, he started to become anxious. Did something happen to his wife-to-be? Did she miss the train altogether? Did she get off at the wrong stop? Or did she decide to jilt him? He heard of it happening to other men who placed adverts. Women would start with one destination in mind, but along their travels find a better offer, and ditch their intended. Did she decide to do that to him?

When no one else exited the train, James walked over to the train conductor, hoping he might have answers. Maybe he knew what happened to the woman James was going to marry.

"Excuse me, sir, I was wondering if I could ask you about a passenger who was supposed to be on the train."

The man paused from helping the new passengers load onto the train and looked over at James with a skeptical eye. "Give me a moment to finish loading these passengers."

Once the man was finished, he stepped down from the train and gave his attention to James. "What's this all about?"

"I came here to meet my future wife. She was supposed to arrive here today, on this train."

"Everyone who was getting off this train at this stop has disembarked," the man explained. "We only have passengers traveling on to other parts of the country."

"I realize that, but she was set to be here. I can't imagine she wouldn't come. Her name was Cara McGregor. This is her picture," he said, pulling out the photo from his pocket and handing it over to the other man.

"I did see a woman on the train that matches this picture—" he started, causing James to be hopeful and worried at the same time.

"What happened? Where is she?" James interrupted, unable to contain his emotions.

"I'm sorry to tell you, but she jumped from the train several miles back."

"What on earth would cause her to do that?" James asked with incredulousness.

"From what I was told, there was a disagreement with another male passenger. A knife was pulled, accusations were made, and before any of it could be sorted out, she jumped from the train."

"You must be joking," James stated with disbelief. "What would possess her to do something so reckless, especially out here where there's no food or water for miles at a time."

"I agree, but by the time I found out and stopped the train, she had disappeared out of sight. We had no idea where she went, and we had a schedule to maintain."

"A schedule to maintain? Are you telling me my future wife is out in the middle of nowhere, most likely hurt, with not knowing where to go?" James questioned with his voice raising in anger as he spoke each word.

"It's not my job to keep a passenger on the train if they wish to get off," the train conductor stated, furrowing his brows together as he pulled down on his black vest. "If you don't mind, I have to get ready for our departure."

Out of habit, James tipped his hat to the other man before turning around to leave. He made his way back over to his wagon and climbed in.

Bewilderment took hold of James' heart as he wondered what he should do about his intended's situation. He pulled out the letter from Cara, which he had carried with him since he first received it.

Mr. Cassidy,

Let me introduce myself. My name is Cara McGregor and I'm Irish. My parents came to America from Ireland two years before I was born. I grew up in the small town of Hull in Massachusetts until my parents died, which is why I'm looking for a new life out West.

I'm twenty years old, five foot three inches tall, with a slender yet sturdy frame. I have red hair the color of a mountain sunset and hazel eyes to match. I try to be a kind and helpful person, focusing more on others than myself. I'm honest and say what I mean, as I don't see a point in playing coy.

I went to school through primary, so I'm proficient in reading, writing and mathematics, which means I can tutor the children as well as help with any bookkeeping you might need for the farm.

I have never been married, and though I have no children, I've always thought that one day I would be a mother. I promise to care for your children as if they were mine, putting their needs above my own.

When I read your letter, my heart was tugged towards your words. I could sense the urgency in what you wrote. The word need spoke to me. I know you and your children must have loved your wife dearly, and you are skeptical of letting another woman into any of your lives. I'm sure the loss is still profound after such a short time, but let me reassure you, I have no intention of taking her place in your life or your children's. Rather, I would hope that one day you all might make room for me in your hearts and we can find a way to be happy together.

. . .

Yours truly,

   Cara McGregor

P.S. I'm also including a picture to confirm my description.

What he had never admitted, not even to himself, was that her words struck a chord with him as much as his advert did with her. She seemed desperate to start a new life, allowing herself some measure of happiness after her profound loss of her parents. They shared that in common; their grief.

Could he leave her out there, all alone, with no way of finding safety from the elements? The decent man in him knew the answer; he couldn't do that to even an animal, let alone another human being. What's more, the husband in him wanted to protect the woman he planned to marry.

James untied his horse from his wagon, deciding he could make better time searching for her without the added bulk. He could have one of the livery boys deliver it to the farm later.

He mounted his horse and took off towards the

direction from where the train had come. He didn't know if he would be able to find her trail, but if he did, he would thank his days as a tracker in the Army before he got married and settled down.

As he continued along the rail line, he looked for any indication of where the train stopped. If anyone got off and looked for her, there would be plenty of footprints to let him know where a good place to start looking would be.

About five miles away, he found what he was looking for. There were over a half a dozen sets of footprints on both sides of the track, but they didn't branch out more than a few hundred yards. If it took some time for the train to slow down, then her tracks would be further down the rail line than where they searched.

He continued about another mile or so, and found a set of smaller boot prints, which he assumed were his future wife's. He moved along the James River, following the path she must have taken.

The further he went on, the footprints became more zigzagged and disheveled, as if she had been dragging one of her legs behind her. She must have gotten hurt jumping from the train, and bad enough she couldn't walk well anymore. Urgency spurred him on, as he pushed in his heels at the side of his horse, coaxing her to go faster.

About another mile down the river, he found a woman passed out on the edge of the bank. She looked exactly like the picture he carried in his pocket, confirming it was indeed Cara McGregor.

James hopped down from his horse and rushed to her side. He bent beside her, placing his hand to her forehead. She was clammy to the touch, but still warm. Her chest was moving up and down, showing that she was still breathing, which was also a good sign.

His touch must have caused her to momentarily rouse, because her eyes flickered open and she glanced up at him with a startled expression. She jerked away from his touch, whispering, "Who are you? What do you want?"

"It's me, James Cassidy, your intended. I'm here to help you, Cara." He wasn't sure why he used her given name, but he figured under the circumstances, she could forgive him the familiarity; that was if she even remembered him doing it.

"Where, where am I?" she mumbled out before she passed out for a second time.

James did a quick inspection of her injuries, and though she had many bumps, bruises and small scrapes, there was only one festering wound just above her ankle that worried him. He didn't suspect it was life threatening at the moment. If he didn't put some ointment on it and stitch it up right away, it might very well turn that way.

He gently lifted her up into his arms, then shifted her so she was leaning over his shoulder before he mounted his horse with the other arm. He placed her in his lap, letting her small frame lean against his own.

As he stared down at the sleeping beauty, he never would have suspected she could have made it this far with such a severe wound. He'd asked for fortitude and grit, and it seemed Cara McGregor had it in spades.

CHAPTER TWO

Sharp pain jolted Cara from her sleep. She sat up quickly, regretting it the moment she did. Her head started pounding, causing her hand to immediately move towards where the pain was coming from. Her fingertips brushed a piece of cloth covering whatever was the source.

Realizing she had no idea where she was, she glanced around the room. She couldn't make out anything that told her. The room was sparsely decorated with only a bed and a dresser in it, though both were kept nice. There was a wedding picture on the wall, and instantly the image of the man who called himself James Cassidy came to mind.

Didn't she recall him telling her he found her

last night? Was this his house? Where was he? What was going on?

Cara glanced under the sheet and blanket. She was glad to see she was still wearing her dress from the previous day, which meant nothing improper had happened to her while she was unconscious. She didn't think Mr. Cassidy seemed like the sort of man who took advantage of a vulnerable woman, but one could never know for certain.

She pushed the covers off her and swung her legs over the side of the bed. The moment she put weight on her foot though, she immediately regretted it. A sharp pain shot up her leg, causing her to fall back on the bed.

Jumping from the train had been an impulse decision, one Cara didn't think about entirely. She wondered if she had known what type of pain it would have caused, if she would have done it any different. A moment later, she realized she wouldn't have. She was a stubborn Irish woman, and there was no way she was going to end up behind bars for a crime she didn't commit. She would have done the same thing even knowing how bad she'd hurt the day after.

The door burst open, and two children stumbled in one on top of the other. The first in the room was a little boy with blond hair and big blue eyes. The second was a slightly taller girl with brown hair and brown eyes. Though they had different obvious physical features, it was clear they were siblings by the way the boy pushed to get in front of the girl, and the girl's bottom lip pushed out in a pout over his behavior.

"Let me guess, you're. . .Thomas and Becky?" Cara asked, pulling the names from the letter their father had sent her.

Both of them nodded as Thomas said, "I'm the man around here when Pa is out working. That makes me in charge."

"Are you now?" Cara said, trying to suppress the smile that was on the verge of breaking out. "I had no idea who I was talking to. Good morning, sir," she said in a pretend serious tone.

"Good morning, Miss Cara. Pa said we were to call you that until you feel comfortable enough to let us call you Ma. How about it? Do you feel comfortable enough yet?" he asked, plopping down on the bed next to her.

Cara wasn't sure what to make of his request, but before she could answer, a third girl entered the room. She was taller than the other two, with long blonde hair, brown eyes, and a body just starting to form into a young woman's.

"She's never going to be our ma," she stated firmly, narrowing her eyes into a glare. "I don't know why Pa thought it was a good idea to bring you here when I take care of everything Ma used to. We don't need you here."

"That's not true, Susie, you're a horrible cook," Becky declared. "We haven't had a decent meal since Ma…" the little girl's lip trembled before tears started to trickle down her cheeks.

"Great, now look what you did, lady? You went and made my sister cry," Susan said, picking up her sister and guarding her like Cara was the enemy.

"Miss Cara didn't do it, you're cooking made Becky cry," Thomas declared with a scrunched-up face. "It makes all of us want to cry."

Cara wasn't sure what to make of the situation, but she realized she could probably use some help before it turned to all-out war in the room. "Where's your Pa?"

"He's out working, that's why I'm in charge," Thomas said with a sigh and a roll of his eyes. "Do you think she has a bad memory from the bump on her head? I just told her that."

"No, I'm fine, Thomas. I just think I need to talk with your Pa, that's all."

"Don't listen to her, Thomas. She doesn't know what to do with us and she wants Pa to handle it," Susan said through narrowed eyes. "Told you she was never going to measure up to Ma."

At the moment, Cara was beginning to think Susan was right. She didn't think she was up to the task of taking care of these three children. It had only been a few minutes, and she felt overwhelmed. How was she going to manage a lifetime of it?

"That's enough, children," she heard a man's voice bark out before James Cassidy came into view. Then in a kinder tone, he added, "Why don't you go start lunch for everyone, Susan, and take your brother and sister with you."

"See, told you Pa was going to have to handle it," Susan said in a know-it-all tone, putting Becky down, then pulling both children behind her. "And I still end up cooking. I tell you, there's no reason for her to be here. None whatsoever."

"I'm sorry about my children," he apologized with a frown as he sat down by her on the bed. "I wanted you to meet them under better circumstances, but I thought you would be sleeping longer, considering the condition I found you in last night."

"Yes, I can't believe you were even able to find me. How did you do that, by the way?"

"I used to be a tracker in the Army," James explained.

"Really?" Cara asked with surprise. "How long ago?"

"Years, before I was married and had children, but the skills I learned never go away, and sometimes they come in handy."

"They did last night," she said with a nod. "I would have died out there if you hadn't found me."

"What caused you to jump from the train yesterday? It had to be something pretty bad to risk all these injuries," James noted with concern, reaching out and touching the side of her head.

Cara shrank back out of reflex, still shaken from the last man who put his hands on her without warning.

"I'm sorry. I didn't mean to startle you," he said, retracting his hand and letting it fall by his side.

"It's not you," she whispered. "I'm just still so confused and out of sorts over what happened to me on the train. When that man attacked me, and tried to force himself on me, I was so scared. I pulled a knife I carried and threatened to harm him if he didn't leave me alone, but it didn't deter him.

He continued to fight with me until a group of miners came into the car. I thought I would be okay; however, he lied. He said I tried to rob him and pulled a knife on him because I was a thief. I was worried they would put me in jail, so I jumped from the train."

"Why would you think they wouldn't believe you?" James asked with confusion. "You could have reported what happened to the train conductor and later the sheriff, rather than risk your life like that."

Cara didn't want to get into her family history, or how she worried it would have tainted her testimony with everyone. Instead, she gave part of the truth by saying, "I wasn't thinking straight. I reacted out of fear."

"I'm sorry all of this happened to you, but you are safe now," he reassured her. "Why don't you rest, and I'll bring you food once it's ready. If you feel up to it later, there's a wash basin by the bed so you can clean up a bit. I'm sorry I don't have any fresh clothes for you, but I have no idea what the train did with your belongings."

"That's alright. I can make do with this dress until I can figure something out. I'm sure a good wash will make all the difference."

James stood with a nod. "I'll leave you for now

then."

Cara watched as her future husband exited the room. He hadn't sent a picture, only a description in his letter, which didn't do him justice at all. Many women would count themselves lucky to marry such a handsome man, with a lean physique, broad shoulders, and a strong jawline. Added to this his kind nature and thriving farm, James Cassidy was a good match. She just needed to let herself accept that for once, her luck had turned around.

———

James balanced the tray of food in one hand, then softly knocked on his bedroom door with the other.

"Come in," he heard Cara's soft voice say from the other side.

He turned the knob and entered the room. Cara looked in better spirits than she did earlier. She had a clean face and body, and most of the dirty spots on her dress were rubbed clean. She must have taken his offer and used the wash basin. Gone was the dirt and debris that had covered her body, and without it she was even more beautiful, if that were possible.

James didn't want to stare, but he couldn't help

it. Her hazel eyes were the prettiest mixture of gold, brown, and green he had ever seen. It reminded him of the grass on the hills during the changing of the seasons. And her hair, she was right when she described it as akin to a mountain sunset. The hues of red and gold in her mane called out to him, begging him to touch it. He knew that after all she had been through, it wasn't something he should do.

Shaking the thought from his head, he asked, "Are you hungry?"

She glanced at the tray and nodded. "I'm starving. I haven't eaten since yesterday morning on the train."

"I should warn you, Susan tries her best, but she isn't the greatest cook," he said, placing the tray on her lap.

"It takes time, like any other skill. You should have seen me when I was her age. I was a disaster in the kitchen, but over time, my mother helped me learn the skills I needed to keep a proper house. I hope I can do the same for Susan."

"I know she hasn't been the friendliest towards you, so it's kind of you to want to help her."

"I understand what it's like to lose a mother; it's a loss unlike any other. Not a day goes by that I don't miss mine. If I can do anything to make that a little more bearable, I'll try."

The kindness in her gesture made James' heart fill with warmth. He had asked for a woman with kindness, and again, Cara showed she was filled with what he and his children needed. He had doubted if he had made the right decision placing the advert for a mail-order bride, but the more he got to know Cara, the more he was sure he had.

Cara gingerly took a couple spoonfuls of the soup and then winced. "I think I'm eating a little fast. I still hurt all over."

"You're lucky that all that happened to you were some bumps and bruises. You could have really hurt yourself jumping off that train," James stated with concern. "Please promise me you won't do anything that reckless again."

"I won't, I just panicked and didn't think about the consequences. I don't know what would have happened to me if you hadn't found me when you did." Cara adjusted herself in the bed and gestured to her leg. "Thanks, by the way, for stitching up my wound. I noticed the good job you did when I cleaned myself up earlier."

"I was worried it would bleed through the night, so I did the best I could. We don't have doctors out here in the frontier, so we learn to do a lot of basic medical care for ourselves."

"With children, I bet that's a real necessity."

James nodded. "Especially with a boy like Thomas. He tends to get into a lot of trouble."

"It sounds like I'll have my hands full with him," Cara stated. "I'll have to keep a close eye."

"Not until you're mended though. The children have strict orders to be on their best behavior until you feel up to getting on your feet again." James paused for a moment, gathering his courage to say the next part. "There is, however, one delicate matter I wish to address."

"What's that?" Cara asked, tilting her head to the side.

"Considering the situation, I was hoping you would understand that we shouldn't be staying in the house together unmarried and need to get married as soon as possible. I had planned on a traveling preacher marrying us today, but with what happened yesterday, I decided to ask him to wait until tomorrow. I don't want to pressure you, but I don't want to set a bad example for the girls or have neighbors wagging their tongues if word gets out that we aren't married yet."

"You have neighbors?"

"Well, yes, not right near, but close enough that word could get around. I wouldn't want any damage done to your reputation."

Cara pressed her lips together as her brows creased in contemplation. A couple moments later, she said, "I don't see a point in waiting. We should go ahead with the wedding tomorrow."

"Why don't you get some sleep in the meantime," James suggested, standing up from the edge of the bed. "I'll put the food over here in case you want any more during the night."

"Where are you going to sleep?"

"I shared Thomas' bed with him in his room last night, but considering you're awake and doing better, I should sleep in the barn until we're married. If you need anything the girls' room is right next door, so just call out and Susan can help you."

"Thank you," Cara whispered, "but I hate displacing you out of your own bed."

"It's not a problem. You need the comfort of it, and I've slept in far worse conditions when I was in the Army. I'll manage just fine."

James headed to the door and exited the room, realizing that come tomorrow, he would be a married man again.

CHAPTER THREE

Screams woke Cara from her sleep the following morning. Startled, she jerked up from the bed, instantly regretting the movement. Though she felt better than the day before, she was still sore. She suspected she would be for days.

Ignoring the pain, she quickly climbed out of the bed and put her skirt and blouse back on over her shift. She pulled on her boots, then pinned back her unruly curls into a bun, wanting to be prepared for whatever was going on in the other part of the house to cause such screams.

Cara walked down the hall and into utter chaos. Smoke was billowing from the kitchen with Thomas running around screaming they were all going to die. Becky was curled up on one of the kitchen table chairs crying into her knees while Susan was frantically trying to fan the smoke away.

"What's going on? What's burning?" Cara inquired, coming up beside the eldest Cassidy child and looking at the stove.

"I've made pancakes and bacon a dozen times before. I don't know what went wrong," Susan mumbled with tears streaming down her cheeks. "Pa is going to be so mad. The house is going to smell like burnt pancakes for days."

"Oh, I don't think he will be," Cara stated, trying to comfort the girl, though she wondered if he was the type of man that got easily angered. If he did, how did he handle it? Was he the type to fly off the handle and hit whoever was around, or did he quietly seethe and punish with silence? She wasn't sure she wanted to find out. "We can fix this before he gets back."

Turning to Thomas, she reached out to stop him from running around. "Thomas, where is your pa by the way?" hoping to distract the boy from making the chaotic situation worse.

"One of the horses was having a baby, so Pa had to go help her," Thomas said, then glancing over the smoke he added, "We're all going to die,

Miss Cara. Susan is going to kill us with her cooking."

Susan whipped around and glared at her brother. "You take that back. If it wasn't for me, you'd starve to death."

"No, that's not true. Miss Cara is here now," Thomas stated, sticking out his tongue for effect. "She'll take care of me."

"Thomas, that isn't a nice thing to say to your sister. She's worked very hard to take care of you and Becky over the past several months. You should be grateful for a sister who can do all that she does," Cara kindly rebuked. "Why don't you go sit down with Becky at the table while I help Susan with breakfast."

Cara turned back to the stove and decided the blackened food was a lost cause. She picked up a rag, wrapped it around the handle of the pan, and lifted it up, then walked over to the door that led out onto the back porch. She found a bucket and scraped the contents into it, then took the bucket outside and set it by the wall. She would deal with it later.

Once back in the house, she came over to Susan's side, where she was leaning against the cabinets with her arms folded across her chest. "I don't know what went wrong. I've never burned anything that bad before," the girl chastised herself.

"It happens, Susan. Mistakes are part of learning. Believe me, I've made plenty," Cara stated, giving the girl an encouraging smile. "Nothing you've done can be worse than the time I actually caught my mother's tablecloth on fire."

"You did?" Susan asked, her eyebrows arching in shock.

Cara nodded. "I was arranging candles on the table—stupidly with the wicks lit—and knocked one over. If my mother hadn't rushed in and put it out with a bucket of water, the whole house would have burned down."

"I guess this isn't that bad," Susan said gesturing around at the smoke and mess in the kitchen.

"No, not at all, and we can air out the house, clean up the kitchen, and start over on breakfast. You'll see, it'll be fine."

"Thanks, Miss Cara," Susan said, then she must have realized she was giving credit to Cara because she quickly added, "I'm not saying I couldn't have handled all of this on my own though."

"Oh, I know you could, but why should you have to with me here. I need to pull my own weight anyway," Cara said, trying to repress the mirth she felt over the girl's stubborn determination to not accept her.

At least not yet; Cara would work on winning Susan over, because despite all of the girl's obstinate ways, Cara liked her. Her feistiness reminded Cara of herself.

"Why don't you open up the windows and doors to air the house out and then clean the pan," Cara suggested. "Let me check on Becky while you do that."

Cara made her way over to the small girl and knelt down beside her. "Are you all right, Becky?"

The little girl peeked over her knees, her bottom lip trembling as she whispered, "I thought the house was going to burn down, and we were all going to die like Ma did."

"No, my darling, that won't happen," Cara said, wrapping her arms around the girl. "I'm here now, and I'll keep you safe."

Once Becky was calm and both the other chores were finished by Susan, they started over on breakfast. Cara watched as Susan made the pancake batter, giving small suggestions through the process. They put the first two measures of pancake batter into the pan, then placed the bacon in the second one.

"An easy way to know when a pancake is ready to flip is when little bubbles start to form in the batter on top," Cara explained, taking the flat wooden utensil and giving an example of how to do it. "Why don't you flip the next one."

Susan took the utensil, and holding it the way Cara had, flipped the pancake perfectly.

"Exactly, that was great, Susan," Cara stated with a smile. "See, you're learning all my secrets. Soon, you'll be a better cook than all the girls in South Dakota."

"That's gonna take a lot of work," Thomas observed from the table.

Cara leaned over and whispered to Susan, "Just ignore him. Boys like to tease. It's what they do. It just means they secretly care."

Susan nodded, whispering back, "Thomas must really care a bunch then."

Cara let out a chuckle, amused by Susan's remark. Susan looked over at her, then let out a small laugh of her own.

"What, what's so funny?" Thomas asked from the other side of the room.

"Oh, it's nothing," Cara said, wanting to keep the secret between her and Susan. "Just a joke amongst us girls."

A half hour later, the four of them were sitting around the table getting ready to eat breakfast.

"Should one of you go get your pa?" Cara inquired, glancing towards the door.

The children shook their heads.

"Pa will eat when he gets back in. He doesn't like being bothered when he's working," Thomas explained, reaching out to take a bite of his bacon from his plate.

Cara gently reached out and tapped his hand. "Not yet. Let's pray first."

Everyone bowed their heads and Cara said, "Dear Lord, we thank you for this day and the food you have provided for us. We pray you bless it to our bodies. In Jesus' Name, we pray, Amen."

The children dove into their meals, gobbling it up like starving animals. Cara suspected they hadn't behaved like this when their mother was alive. How could they have regressed so badly? She supposed if a man was doing the rearing alone, he wouldn't put an emphasis on table manners being important in the grand scheme of things.

Cara used a firm but soft voice to correct the behavior. "Children, is this how we eat our meals properly?"

Both girls stopped what they were doing and

looked over at her while Thomas continued eating, then said with his mouth full, "What are you talking about, Miss Cara?"

"First off, we don't talk with our mouths full," she said, reaching out and gently closing his mouth with her hand. "Secondly, we use one hand with our utensils, like this," she said, giving an example of how to eat with manners.

The girls immediately started to copy her, but Thomas' face turned red as he glared at Cara. "You can't tell me what to do," he yelled, his mouth still full of food.

"With your pa away, I certainly can," she corrected.

"No, you can't! You're not my ma!" he yelled at Cara, jumping up from the table and storming off towards the bedrooms.

Cara wasn't sure what to do, but she knew she couldn't let him get away with how he was behaving. If the children thought she was willing to let them behave in such a poor manner, then complete anarchy would rule the house. They would all be defying her in short order.

Standing up from the table, Cara made her way down the hall and entered Thomas' room. He was on the ground, rolling a baseball against the wall.

"Thomas, what was that all about? I thought we were getting along quite splendidly, up until breakfast time."

When he continued to ignore her, Cara picked up the ball to get his attention.

"Give me back my ball!" he bellowed, rushing up to her and trying to yank it out of her hand.

"No, not until we're done talking," Cara explained. "We need to figure out what is going on."

"You're not my ma, that's what's going on," he shouted at her, still trying to take the ball. When she stepped back from him, he reached out and grabbed her arm, then pulled it to his mouth.

A sharp pain shot up her arm, and Cara realized that Thomas had bit her! She jerked back, pulling her arm from his mouth. A giant red mark with teeth imprints were visible in the center of her forearm.

"You bit me, Thomas! You can't go around biting people just because you're angry," she stated with shock and anger, pressing her free hand against the wound. "You are going to stay in this room on your bed and think about what you just did."

Cara took the ball with her and exited the room, pulling the door shut behind her.

She thought Thomas was the one Cassidy child on her side, and now she wasn't even sure of that. Had she taken on more than she could handle, coming out West to be these children's new mother? She'd always gotten along well with the children in her own town but trying to win these three over was something else.

As she went about the chores of cleaning up the kitchen, she silently sent up a prayer to God asking Him for His help. She knew she was going to need it.

———

The smell of burnt food still lingered in the house when James entered later that morning. None of the children were present, and Cara was drying the last of the dishes.

"There's a plate of pancakes and bacon under a napkin on the table," Cara stated, turning around to tell him. She moved to the side to place a dish on a shelf, when she winced, stumbling a tiny bit.

"Should you be doing all this work with your leg still healing?" James inquired with concern. "It can't be good to be standing on it for long periods of time."

Cara shrugged. "I can manage, Mr. Cassidy."

"Since we're getting married today, I think you can start calling me James."

"I suppose that makes sense. You should probably call me Cara then as well."

"All right, Cara, shouldn't Susan and Becky be helping you?"

"I haven't been standing that much. Susan helped me cook and after we ate, they asked to go read."

James made a sniffing sound, saying, "Well, that explains the smell."

"Please, don't mention it to Susan. She's sensitive about the incident, and I barely got her to calm down a bit ago."

"It's sweet you want to protect her," James said, taking a seat at the table and pulling the plate towards him. "I'll make sure to keep my lips sealed about the odor."

Cara came over and took a seat next to him. "I need to talk with you about Thomas."

James let out a heavy sigh, placing his fork down and giving his attention to Cara. "What did he do this time?"

"He had a tantrum during breakfast. I'm not sure what caused it. Perhaps my gentle correction, or it could be the stress of having someone new in the house, but he stormed off to his room. When I went to see what happened, he yelled at me and bit my arm."

"He what?" James growled out in disbelief. Glancing over at her, he scanned her body for the evidence, his eyes landing on the spot on her right arm. "I'll go take care of this right now."

As James went to stand from the table, Cara reached out to stop him, placing her hand on his arm. "You don't need to be harsh with him. He's having a break in his room, where I asked him to think about what he did."

"You're sure that's how to handle it?" James asked, sitting back down in his chair.

"I'm no expert in the matter, but I think that he's just acting out due to all the changes. I think once he's had time to think about it, he'll have remorse over what he did. He's a sweet boy under all the roughness."

"I have to say, I marvel at how much kindness you can muster for my children, considering how much testing they have done in just one day."

"Why don't you finish your breakfast while I go talk to Thomas."

James nodded, then took a bite of the perfect

pancake. His eyes grew wide with appreciation. After swallowing, he said to her retreating figure, "This is excellent. You must have made it."

She stopped moving and smiled. "Actually, it was Susan, with my guidance."

"You're already making a marked improvement around here," he said, before trying the crisp bacon, which was equally delicious.

"Thank you," she said, then glancing at his clothes, she added, "You should probably get cleaned up after you eat. We're getting married after all."

"I'm sorry you don't have a different dress to wear," James stated with a frown. "If we had time, I would make the trip into town to get you one."

"It's not your fault that I ended up leaving my belongings on the train. Besides, it's not the clothes I will miss as much as the pictures of my parents and my mother's jewelry."

"I'm sorry. I suppose we could write to the railway company and ask them to send on your belongings to us," James suggested.

"Considering how things ended, I don't want to kick that hornet's nest. It's best just to count the items as lost."

"Still, I know as a woman, you would've liked to be married in a new dress, or at least a fresh one. I promise, once things settle down around here, we'll make a trip into town and get you some new clothes."

"I'll hold you to that promise," she said with a wink. "This dress will only last so long."

Cara turned back around and disappeared down the hall, leaving James alone.

As he ate his breakfast, he contemplated if he was making the right decision by offering Cara a chance to be married. Was he being selfish trying to fix his broken home through marrying another woman? Was his choice to remarry helping or harming his children? He wasn't sure, considering how they were behaving, but he had given Cara his word that he would marry her. He couldn't very well go back on it now that she'd traveled all this way. James was going to have to find a way to make this work.

Silently, he sent up a prayer asking God to guide him on this new path for his life. He wasn't sure how to navigate it, but knew God was capable of doing the steering for him.

By the end of the meal and prayer, James was feeling much better about the situation. He took his plate and cleaned it at the sink, then placed it on the wooden rack to dry.

He padded down the hall and was grateful to hear laughter coming from Thomas' room. He pushed the door open to find Cara sitting on the edge of his son's bed, both of them laughing at a book she held in her hands.

"Miss Cara is reading me a story about the jungle. The monkey is so funny in it, Pa."

"I'm glad to see everyone is getting along again," James stated with a grin. "I'll leave you to the story then, while I go get cleaned up for the wedding."

James slipped away and headed down the hall to his bedroom. He entered and washed up at the basin before walking over to his armoire where he pulled out a white button-up cream shirt and pair of dark brown pants. He slipped the clothes on, then combed his hair into place, before heading back into the living room where everyone was gathered, dressed in their Sunday outfits.

A knock at the door drew everyone's attention to the front of the house. James walked over and opened the door to find a tall, thin man with balding gray hair standing on the other side. He was dressed in a wrinkled black suit and carrying a small tapestry bag.

"You must be the preacher," James said, stepping back to let the other man enter the house.

"Indeed I am. Theodore Demont at your service," he said, entering the room and looking at the occupants. "I see you managed to get yourself a looker."

James didn't know how to respond to that. It seemed odd to hear a preacher say something like that, but he'd never spent any time with a traveling one. Avoiding a response, James said instead, "I think we'll have the ceremony over by the fire."

James walked over to the hearth and waited for everyone to join him.

The preacher arrived right behind him, pulled out a Bible from his tapestry bag, and made a clearing noise in his throat before saying, "There's the matter of the fee."

"Oh, yes," James mumbled, pulling out money from his pocket. He handed it over to the other man, who put the money in his pocket, and then opened the Bible in his hands.

"Now that that's settled, let's get this wedding underway."

Cara came over and joined James in front of

the hearth. They turned to face each other as the children came to stand next to them.

"You're both sure you want this?" he asked, glancing down to the Bible in his hands and back up to them.

Both James and Cara nodded.

"Okay then, we're gathered here to unite these two people in marriage. Do you…." He looked at James and scratched his head. "What did you tell me your name was when I came through a couple of weeks ago?"

"James Cassidy," he said, then adding, "and this is Cara McGregor, like I told you."

"Yes, yes, I remember now. Do you, James Cassidy, take Cara McGregor to be your wedded wife?"

"I do," James stated.

"You're sure?" the preacher asked a second time.

"I am," James stated firmly, trying to hide the irritation he was beginning to feel for the man.

"All right, and do you, Cara McGregor, take James Cassidy to be your wedded husband?"

Cara lowered her head, then quietly said, "I do."

"And you're sure?" he repeated with a doubtful

tone in his voice. "I can't tell when you aren't looking at me. You need to be sure."

"I'm sure," Cara stated, raising her head up and looking directly at the preacher.

"I guess that works," he muttered under his breath as he looked down at the book again. "Do you have the rings?"

"Yes, right here," James said, pulling two gold bands from his pocket.

"Let me have them then," the preacher demanded.

"Why?" James asked with confusion, never having the preacher who married him to his first wife make the request.

"I'm doing the marrying around here. Don't ask why."

Repressing a sigh that was threatening to erupt, James handed the rings over to the preacher. He placed them in the center of his Bible and laid his hands over them. He mumbled something under his breath, which James thought might be a prayer of blessing. The preacher picked them back up, but before he could hand them over, he dropped them on the ground. "My apologies, my apologies," he said shutting his book and then bending down to grab the items.

James bent down to help, but the preacher grabbed the rings before James could do anything. As they both went to stand up, their heads collided.

"Ouch!" the preacher screamed. "What are you trying to do? Kill a man of God?"

"No, sir, no, I didn't mean to do that."

The preacher stepped back a couple of steps, rubbing his head. "I'm going to stay back here from now on." Then he reached out and gave a ring to James. "Place this ring on her finger."

James took the ring from the preacher's outstretched hand and did as he was ordered. But to his surprise it wouldn't fit. "Did you give me the right ring?"

"Hand it back over," the preacher said with irritation. "You must have caused me to mix them up when you hit me in the head."

James wanted to correct the preacher's statement but figured what was the point. The man was clearly confused about the whole situation. He gave the ring to the preacher, who took it, switched the rings around and returned it.

"Try putting it on again, then repeat after me, with this ring, I thee wed."

Luckily, this time the ring fit. James repeated the

words, then Cara placed her ring on James' finger and said the same vow.

"I now pronounce you married," the preacher said, slamming his Bible shut. "It's done."

Cara's eyes grew round as she glanced from the preacher to James. He could tell she was as shocked by the abrupt ending as he was.

"I have to go," the preacher said, heading straight for the door. "More weddings to perform and all."

Before anyone could say anything, the man vanished from the house, leaving the newly formed family standing awkwardly around the hearth.

"That guy was so weird," Thomas declared, heading over to the sofa to take a seat. "But I guess we got a new ma now, so that's all that matters."

"Can I go to my room?" Susan asked with a frown on her face. "I want to take a nap."

"Of course, Susan," James stated. "I'll have Cara get you when it's time to help her with the wedding meal."

"Wedding meal?" Cara inquired, her brows furrowing together with confusion. "Are we celebrating?"

"I thought it would be nice," James stated, a little shocked she didn't think there was a need to celebrate their union. "I've saved one of my best pigs for tonight."

"What do you mean? Why did you save it?"

"So I could slaughter it for the dinner. Don't worry, I'll bring the slabs inside the kitchen for you so you can butcher them into more manageable pieces."

"Wait, what? You expect me to butcher it?" Cara squeaked out with disbelief. "I've always gotten my meat from the butcher shop. I have no idea what I'm doing."

"It's easy to figure out. If you've seen butchered meat at the shop, you know what they should look like. I would help you, but I have to tend to the crops. If I don't keep up on them, they won't be ready for harvest at the end of the summer."

As James headed out of the house and over to the barn, he tried to make peace with the odd wedding that just took place. He hoped it wasn't a sign that the marriage would be as big as a disaster as the ceremony.

CHAPTER FOUR

Cara tried to wrap her mind around what just happened. She was a married woman now, a result of the most peculiar wedding she had ever seen. She supposed it could be because he was a traveling preacher and had to marry lots of couples he didn't know. Something didn't set well with her about him or the way he conducted their wedding.

It didn't matter though, she had to make peace with the fact that the deed was done. This was her new life and she had to figure out a way to make it work, starting with butchering a pig.

Cara pressed her lips together as she stared at the giant slabs of meat sitting in front of her. She tried not to think about the fact the animal had been alive just a couple of hours ago, enjoying itself in the barn, or that at one time he had been a cute little piglet, running around the farm without a care in the world. All that changed when the poor creature met the end of James' knife. Now, she was tasked with the deplorable job of making him into meals. What she wouldn't give to be back in Hull where she could ask the butcher to give her pork chops and cutlets with a side of bacon. *Where does bacon even come from?* she wondered as she turned the meat over.

Susan came out and stood next to Cara. "Ma used to do this, then Pa took over once she was gone."

"Do you know what I'm supposed to do?" Cara asked, hopeful for help.

"I've never done it, and quite honestly, I don't like being around when it happens," Susan confessed with a shudder. "I can't keep from thinking about it being a piglet a year ago."

"Me too," Cara agreed with a sigh, "but your Pa insists I can do it, so I'll have to try."

Cara started with the cuts she thought she could figure out the easiest, like the chops, shoulder, and ribs, but she had no idea how to figure out where the loin, ham, or bacon came from.

By the time she ended the process, the kitchen

looked like a massacre had taken place in it. She was sweating profusely and tired beyond belief. All she wanted to do was go lay down, but she still had to put the meat away, clean up, and prepare the wedding meal.

At least she had Susan for that. She tasked the girl with making the side dishes of rice and peas. They had bread leftover from the day before, so all that was left was for Cara to clean up and then cook the meat. She set about the work, trying to ignore the pain radiating up her leg from her wound. It was healing, but it was going to be a while before she was able to do all she used to be able to do comfortably, but she didn't want James or the children to know that.

Cara pushed through the pain and was grateful once all of her chores were finally done. She had Becky set the table while she sent Thomas out to fetch their pa.

Relief flooded her body as she took a seat at the table, glad that the last dish was complete. She could rest, at least until after the meal and the dishes needed to be done.

James and Thomas entered the house a few minutes later and joined them at the table after washing up.

"This looks good," James said with a grin, his eyes moving from dish to dish until they came to rest on the meat. His head tilted to the side as he inquired, "Are those pork chops?"

"Yes, they are," Cara stated defensively. "Why is something wrong?"

He shook his head. "No, I'm sure they taste great."

Everyone heaped portions of the food onto their plates and then James said a prayer over the meal.

Cara watched as the family dug into the food, hoping that everyone was happy with what she and Susan made. Her first moments of concern came when she noticed everyone, even James, had a difficult time cutting into the meat, almost as if they were sawing away at a piece of wood that wouldn't budge. The next moment of apprehension surfaced when they finally got pieces of pork to their mouths, and she realized it was taking them far longer than it should to chew each bite.

"What's wrong with this meat?" Thomas asked, trying to swallow the meat before he spoke, but she could tell it wasn't going down easy.

"And you thought my cooking was bad," Susan

stated snidely. "I'm only twelve. What's her excuse?"

"Susan, that wasn't polite," James choked out, picking up his glass of sun tea and taking a big gulp. "Besides, it's not her cooking as much as the cut of the meat that caused the problem. I should have butchered the meat for her rather than put that responsibility on her when she wasn't ready."

Cara felt embarrassed over her lack of being able to handle the situation. She wanted to please her new husband, but it seemed she had failed miserably.

The exhaustion and disappointment from the day took over, causing Cara to jump to her feet and rush from the room. She could feel her legs tremble beneath her, threatening to collapse at any moment, but she forced herself to keep going until she reached the bed, throwing herself on it.

She buried her face in the pillow, angry at herself for not being able to perform the duties James expected of her. If she couldn't even butcher a pig right, how would she be able to do all the other chores correctly?

Earlier in the day, Susan had rattled off the list of what the girls and James did now since her ma passed away. It was long and full of tasks Cara had no idea how to manage. She'd thought she would be able to cope once she was healed up, but now she doubted if she would be able to accomplish any of it, especially to the level the Cassidy family needed. Had she made a mistake promising to be a wife and mother to these people?

Tears stung her eyes and wet the pillow, causing it to cling to her, making it hard to breathe, but she didn't dare turn over. She didn't want any of them to hear her cry. Her Irish pride wouldn't allow that.

Unable to hold it in any longer, she let the sobs out in big, raking heaps. Not only from the failure of dinner, but over the frustration of the wedding ceremony, what happened with Thomas, and how Susan treated her with contempt. She didn't know if she could live her life feeling like an outsider with a family she was supposed to take care of. It had only been a couple of days, but it felt like an eternity already. How would she actually make it a week? A month? A lifetime?

———

James was still staring down the hall where Cara just disappeared. What was he supposed to do about what just happened? He self-admittedly didn't deal with outbursts of emotions well. It was why he had such a hard time with Susan lately. She was always getting upset about something, and it grated on his nerves. He didn't very well need *two* women in his house behaving like this. What was he going to do about it?

"Children, I'm going to check on Miss Cara."

"You think that's a good idea? It never is when Susan's mad," Thomas pointed out.

James worried his son was right, but he didn't think it would go over any better if he left her alone. He needed to at least try to let her know he didn't like seeing his wife upset.

He trudged down the hallway like a man being led to a firing squad. He was not looking forward to the tears and accusations he was sure would follow when he entered his bedroom. It felt like he was entering into a battlefield rather than a sanctuary at this point.

Rather than just entering, softly he knocked on the door. "Can I come in?"

When there was no response, he inhaled a deep breath, twisted the knob, and entered. Cara was curled up on the bed with her face hidden in a pillow. He walked over and took a seat next to her.

"I just want to say: I realize now I made a

mistake by putting that all on you. It was unfair to tell you to just figure it out on your own. I should have shown you."

Cara remained still and didn't say a word. She was being silent with him as a punishment. He recognized the move from his first wife, who had been an expert at doing it.

"I understand if you don't want to speak right now; if you need to feel better before you want to talk." James started to reach out to put his hand on her back but decided it might make her more upset. He let his hand drop to his side, then continued. "How about in the morning, we go over the chores around the house, and anything you don't know how to do, I can help you find the best way to do them."

When he still didn't get a response, he decided it was best if he just left her alone for the night. Hopefully, she would feel better in the morning.

James exited his bedroom and entered Thomas' room next door. His son was already in bed, reading a book before it was time to go to sleep. He looked up at his father and asked, "Why aren't you sleeping with Miss Cara tonight like you did with Ma? You're married now."

"Yes, but she's upset, and I don't want to make it worse by pushing her to let me do that."

That was only part of it. The truth was, James wasn't sure when Cara would feel comfortable enough to let him sleep in the same room as her. They were relatively strangers after only knowing each other two days, plus considering she was attacked on the train, he didn't want to disrespect her privacy. There was also the issue that though he found Cara attractive, he was still in love with his dead wife. It wasn't fair, and he knew it, but the idea of being intimate with any other woman made him feel like he was betraying Laura. He just wasn't ready to take that step, and he wasn't sure if he would ever be.

As his son drifted off to sleep next to him, James sent up a silent prayer, asking God to help him figure out the way to make his marriage work.

CHAPTER FIVE

The sunshine floating through the window, along with the birds chirping outside, ushered in the new morning. Cara stretched out, waking her body from its slumber. After a couple moments of sending up a prayer for God to help her, she climbed out of bed, determined to do better today. She was going to find a way to be the best wife and mother to the Cassidy family.

Cara slipped on her one and only dress, pulled a comb through her hair, and marched out of the bedroom and straight to the kitchen. To her surprise, breakfast was already made and James and the children were waiting at the table for her.

"You woke just in time. I was about to go get you," James stated with a warm smile. "I didn't want to wake you early, but you're going to need a hardy breakfast for our outing today."

"Our outing?" Cara questioned, her eyebrow arching in puzzlement.

"I think it's time we head into town and get you some new clothes. While we're there, we can have a doctor take a look at your wound, make sure everything is healing well, and get any ointments we might need to help it along."

"Thank you," Cara said, taking a seat as her heart filled with gratitude.

James had promised to get her some new clothes, but she honestly thought it might be several more days before it happened. The idea of seeing a real doctor did appeal to her. Though she didn't want to admit it, her leg was bothering her something awful.

"I need to take care of my new wife," he said with a nod. "We all want you in tip-top shape around here."

And there it was. He wanted her fit to work, and figured she was shallow enough that a few pretty dresses and bonnets would make her forget all about how awful the past couple of days had been. He didn't know her very well.

"I'll have you know, Mr. Cassidy, I'm not distracted by expensive, new clothes."

"It's Mr. Cassidy again? I thought we were at least past formalities by now. What's going on, Cara?"

"I think you should address me as *Miss* Cara, considering this is more of a business arrangement than a marriage," she stated tartly.

The smile vanished from his face as he slammed his fists down on the table. "I don't know how to win with you. Everything I do seems to make things worse."

The words stung, but Cara forced herself not to react. She desired James to want her as a real wife, in every sense of the word, but she doubted he was capable. She suspected he was still in love with his dead wife, and if that was the case, she had no hope of having a real marriage.

Defensively, she retorted, "That's the problem with you, Mr. Cassidy. You think this is about winning. That couldn't be further from the truth, but if that's how you want it, then we can have it your way. From now on, let's keep the boundaries and duties clear. I am your wife, in name only. I will do all the duties a good frontier mother and wife needs to do, outside the bedroom. That is one area that is strictly off-limits."

James crossed his arms and narrowed his eyes. "If that's how you want it."

"It is," she stated firmly, turning around to leave the room.

Before she could escape though, Thomas' voice stopped her in her tracks. "Wait, don't we need Miss Cara to make us a bath? Ma used to always do it."

"Thomas, that's not appropriate to ask of her," James snapped out.

"It's only a bath, Pa. We're all really dirty, especially you. What's wrong with that?" the little boy protested in innocence, apparently completely unfazed by the newly married couple's first fight.

James looked uncomfortable. Cara debated about letting him squirm a little longer, but she could see Thomas was getting angry because he wasn't getting his way. Another fit was the last thing she needed. "It's fine, Mr. Cassidy. I can draw a bath for everyone to use, since it sounds like it is one of my many duties. The water pump is just outside the house, correct?"

"It is, but with your ankle still swollen, I think

you should refrain from getting the water. At least let me help you with that."

Cara nodded, standing up from the table. She didn't like accepting his help, but the idea of carrying in several heavy buckets of water seemed like a daunting task, given her current physical condition.

"I'll put the tub by the fire," James stated, heading towards the pantry where it was stored. "Then I'll be outside to help with the buckets."

She nodded before leaving the kitchen and headed out the back to the pump. As she watched the liquid pour into the bucket, the cool water did little to mitigate the fuming rage she felt inside her heart. Cara hated the fact that James was treating her more like a maid than a wife. When she agreed to get married to a stranger, she had no idea he could and would treat her in such a way. She felt like she didn't matter more than what he could get from her. What could she do to let him see how that made her feel?

An idea sprang to mind. If he thought she was nothing more than a business arrangement, she was going to show him what it would cost him to treat her as such. When they got to Mitchell, she was going to get the most expensive dresses and bonnets the town had to offer. That would teach him!

James came out back and took the first bucket from Cara. Without a word, he turned around and went back in the house. Good, she didn't want to talk to him either.

Five buckets later, and the bathtub was filled to the necessary height.

"Whose first?" Cara asked standing next to the tub, waiting for someone to answer her.

"Pa always goes first," Susan stated with authority. "Then the rest go after."

"You don't need me for this, do you?" she said, more as a statement than a question.

He shook his head. "I'm fully capable of undressing and bathing myself."

"But Ma always helped you with that too," Thomas protested.

Cara's head jerked to stare at the little boy. If she didn't know any better, she would think he was purposely trying to make things more awkward than they already were.

"That's enough, Thomas," James stated sternly. "You and your sisters go outside and play until I'm finished."

The children did as they were ordered, leaving Cara and James alone.

"I'll go clean the kitchen," she said, not wanting to wait around to see how tempting he looked with his shirt off. It didn't matter, he wasn't interested in her that way anyhow.

Without waiting to hear his response, she hurried off before the first set of buttons were undone on his shirt.

Halfway through finishing the dishes, she heard James' voice call from the other room, "Miss Cara, are you there?"

She debated about answering, thinking a good ignoring was exactly what he deserved, but in the end, she answered. "Yes, what is it?"

"You forgot to bring me a towel. I can't dry off without one."

Could she ask Susan or Becky to do it? Somehow, she found that inappropriate to ask girls of their age to do that for their father. There was no way she could ask Thomas, as he would probably wander off and never return with a towel. She supposed she could leave James to get out and find one on his own, but then that would just create a dripping mess that she would end up having to clean up. It was just better to give in and get him a towel, no matter how uncomfortable it made her.

"I'll be right there. Just let me get one from the clothesline," she said, leaving the kitchen and heading out back.

A few moments later, she returned with the towel. She made her way over to the hearth and held out the piece of cloth.

She knew she should try to avert her eyes, but his bare chest beckoned to be looked upon. His golden skin glistened under the water, the soap bubbles covering just enough to keep his modesty intact, part of her wishing it wasn't the case. She wondered what it would be like to touch his chest with her hand. Would it feel rough from all the labor, or would it be soft like the feathers of a duck? Would the muscles ripple under her fingertips?

Her eyes drifted from his body to his face, and his knowing grin made it obvious that he knew what she was thinking. "Like what you see?"

Her cheeks flamed red with embarrassment as she quickly dropped the towel next to the tub and rushed from the room. She wasn't sure how it was possible, but her husband might possibly be the most infuriating man she'd ever met.

Two hours later, the children were bathed and

dressed, the tub was emptied, cleaned and stored, and they were ready to go into town.

The hour ride might have been the bumpiest and hot one Cara ever encountered, making it unpleasant for her as she felt every bit on her still-healing body. When they finally reached Main Street, she was never so grateful to climb down from a wagon.

"I think we should head over to the doctor's office first," James suggested, "then finish up with shopping."

Cara didn't respond, just allowing James to lead the way, after giving a slight nod of her head.

The doctor's visit was short and quick. The older gentleman was friendly and asked a lot of questions, not only about her injuries but her personal situation. Cara tried to answer without going into much detail.

She left with a fresh jar of ointment for the wound and orders to keep her physical activity to a minimum for the next week. She wanted to snort, knowing that wasn't going to happen around the Cassidy house. She refrained, knowing it wouldn't go over well with either the doctor or her new husband.

Next, they picked up some supplies and provisions for the house at the mercantile before heading to their final stop at the dress shop.

"Why don't you go ahead and pick out what you need," James directed Cara. Giving a nod to the owner of the store, he added, "This is my new wife, so make sure to get her whatever she asks."

Cara began to walk around the store, touching the soft edges of several dresses made from various fabrics and in multiple colors. The styles of the dresses weren't quite as in fashion as what she had been used to back in Hull—a momentary pang of sadness crept into her heart over the loss of her own items—but she had to make do with what was available.

She immediately knew that the heavier, velvet dresses with brocade and the satin ones with lace and embroidery trim were the most expensive in the store. She also knew the matching bonnets would make James' wallet hurt.

Cara picked up the hat she suspected was the most expensive in the store and slipped it on her head, securing it with the blue ribbons that came down on both sides.

"That looks pretty on you," James stated from the side of her.

"We have a mirror right over here," the store

owner stated with a wide grin, realizing that Cara was indeed in the store to spend money.

Everyone around her was gushing over how gorgeous the hat looked on her, but all Cara could think about was that her plan to make James pay didn't make her feel any better about her situation. She took off the hat and placed it back on display.

It wasn't like her to give into evil intent, and she wasn't going to start now. She refused to start her marriage off by bankrupting her husband out of spite.

Quickly, she picked out two of the cheapest work outfits, one church dress, and a bonnet with a couple of changeable ribbons to save money. She handed the items over to the store owner, who's smile had diminished slightly when she realized that Cara wasn't going to spend the type of money she first thought.

"Is that all you're getting?" James inquired with surprise.

"Yes, I don't need much," Cara explained.

James shrugged, pulling out a wad of money and handing several bills over to the store owner to cover the cost.

They exited the store and headed back to the wagon where the children were waiting.

"Hold on, I forgot something back at the shop," James stated. "Why don't you wait here with the children."

James scampered across the road, leaving her with the girls who were reading, and Thomas who was playing with his ball again.

Cara looked around the town, trying to find something to distract her from the emptiness she felt inside. She wasn't sure why she felt so melancholy, many women were in far worse situations than her. It didn't help that despite all her best attempts to come into the marriage ready to have a sterile relationship, she wanted more: more from James, more from herself, and more from life.

"Excuse me, miss, but I think I recognize you from the other day," she heard a man say from beside her.

Cara turned towards the unfamiliar voice and found a face she didn't recognize. "I'm sorry, but I don't think you know me."

"Oh, but I think you do. Aren't you the girl that jumped off the train a couple days ago? After you did, the conductor questioned all the passengers to figure out who you were so they could track you down. Didn't you try to rob a man or something?"

"No, I didn't," Cara stated with a mixture of

frustration and fear. "And I'm with my family, so I would appreciate your moving along."

"Your family?" the man asked with confusion, glancing at the children behind her. "I guess I must be mistaken then."

The man started to move away, scratching his head. He stopped and turned back around. "I swear you look just like the girl. I was one car away, but she passed through mine several times."

He narrowed his eyes, stepping close again, as if trying to convince himself she was not who he thought. "You know, they're offering a reward to anyone who can tell where the girl is. I wonder…"

James came up beside them, giving a perplexed look at the other man. "Are you bothering my wife?"

The man stepped back and shook his head. "No, no, I had her confused with someone else."

"We should be going," Cara stated, wanting to get as far away as possible as quickly as they could.

James nodded, helping Cara into the wagon, then climbing up into the driver's seat next to her.

Once they were headed back down the road, he asked, "What was that all about?"

"He thought he recognized me from the train."

"Is that so?"

"It doesn't matter. It's fine," Cara stated, trying to convince herself as much as James. The truth was, Cara was scared. If that man was being honest, then Cara was in real trouble. She needed to stay clear of Mitchell, and every other town from now on.

Wanting to change the subject, Cara asked, "What did you forget at the store?"

"This," he said, pulling a wrapped package from behind the bench. "I was going to wait to give it to you later, but since you asked…"

Cara opened the gift to reveal the velvet bonnet with the blue ribbons she had tried on in the dress shop. "You went back and bought me the hat?" she asked with astonishment, taken aback by the kind gesture.

"I saw how much you liked it, and I figured you didn't want to get it because you thought it was too expensive. I thought you deserved a treat after what you've been through."

"Thank you," Cara whispered, feeling even worse than she did before about how she had behaved earlier.

Perhaps she was wrong about her new husband. Maybe he wasn't as callous as she thought. Maybe he was just the type of man that took a little longer to figure out than others. She could be patient and wait until he was ready to make their marriage something more.

———————

Two weeks had passed, and Cara was settling in well at the farm. She was managing her chores, her leg was healing, and the children seemed to be adjusting to her taking charge. The only area that hadn't progressed was James' relationship with her, but not because of anything she was doing.

They were cordial to one another, but their interaction wasn't going beyond working together for their common goals. James knew that the problem was his fault. He had mixed feelings about letting himself form romantic feelings for Cara, despite the kindness and patience she had shown him over the past couple of weeks.

When she laughed, or smiled at him, he found himself wanting to allow something more to develop with her. When he got up the courage to open his heart, the image of his deceased wife would come to mind. James would feel like he was betraying her, causing him to retract. He wanted to find a way to break through the walls he had around his heart, but he didn't know how.

Letting out a heavy sigh, James looked up into the strong midday sky and wiped the sweat from his brow with the back of his sleeve. It was a boiler of an afternoon, and he needed a break, not to mention a bite to eat.

He took the plow and oxen back to the barn, then headed over to the back of the house where he washed up at the faucet before entering.

Thomas was playing with Becky in the living room while Cara and Susan were in the kitchen cleaning dishes.

"You're just in time to join us," Cara declared.

"Join you doing what?"

His question was answered as Cara turned around with a picnic basket in her hand.

"The family is going to head down to the stream," she explained, giving him a welcoming smile. "The children told me that you used to have picnics there often, but stopped after…" Her words trailed off as she averted her eyes and her cheeks flushed pink with embarrassment.

The awkward moment was interrupted when Thomas burst in between them jumping up and down. "We're going on a picnic, Pa. It's gonna be so much fun."

"It sure will, son," James agreed with a grin, as he reached out and ruffled his son's hair. "Here let me help with that," James offered, taking the wicker basket from Cara.

"My leg's doing much better. I can manage now," Cara pointed out.

"I realize that, but I can still help my wife if I want," he countered with a playful lopsided grin, trying to be as charming as he could be.

"Thank you," she said, following him out the door with the children behind them.

The family walked down to the stream, then followed along the edge until they reached an area where a tiny grass knoll waited.

"This is where we normally have picnics," Susan said, shaking out the folded blanket she had brought along. "We can play in the water after we eat, and it has a perfect view of the sunset."

"You children brought us to the right place. It's perfect," Cara whispered, her face glowing from her excitement.

Everyone took seats on the blanket and Cara opened up the picnic basket. She pulled out and handed cloth napkins to everyone, then pulled out several pots and dishes. Each one revealed something delicious to eat, from freshly made bread with butter and jam, cheese and various fruits, shelled pecans and walnuts, and cured ham. There was also a strawberry cobbler for dessert.

"The food looks and smells wonderful, ladies," James stated with mouth-watering anticipation. "I don't know what I want to try first."

"There's plenty of everything, so start where you'd like," Cara explained, gesturing to the buffet of options.

The kids didn't wait a moment longer and dove right in to picking their favorite items.

Thomas grabbed a bunch of grapes, ham, and a piece of buttered bread. Becky took a peach along with a handful of pecans, always being a light eater. Susan spent a little more time, assembling a sandwich with two pieces of bread, ham and cheese, and an apricot to go with it.

"What would you like to try first?" Cara asked James. "If you want, I could make you a sandwich."

"That would be nice, thank you," James said, appreciative of her unexpected offer.

Cara buttered two pieces of bread, then placed two pieces of ham, layered with two pieces of cheese between them. She handed it over to him.

Next, she gave him a bunch of grapes, and some walnuts.

"You picked all my favorite," James noted with awe. "How did you do that?"

"I've been paying attention to what you like over the past couple of weeks," she said with a wink. "I want to be a good wife and make you happy."

The sweet words and gesture behind them penetrated James' heart, helping to tear down a bit of the wall he'd kept around it since Laura's death.

He took the food and quietly ate it as the children jabbered on about the reading and mathematics lessons Cara had been teaching them. He watched her as she laughed, pushing her curls out of her face, and lovingly corrected their mistakes, explaining the difference between a numerator and denominator once more.

James loved how good Cara was with his children. She was a natural mother, and he wondered what it would be like to have a child of their own. Would she be even more beautiful with her belly round and her face flush from pregnancy? It was hard to imagine her being prettier than she already was, but Laura had been with each of their children.

Laura. Every time he let himself start to imagine a life with Cara beyond a partnership, his deceased wife would creep into the musings and stop him cold in his tracks.

The children finished their food and then begged to go play in the stream.

"Go enjoy yourselves," Cara said, pointing towards the water's edge.

"Come with us," Becky begged.

Cara glanced over at James, who nodded. "You go enjoy yourself too. I'm going to rest right here."

His family jumped up and rushed off. They jumped from one rock to another, splashing water at each other, laughing with joy. It was the perfect picture, his children playing with their new mother.

Cara was like a breath of fresh air, one that they desperately needed after the difficulties in the past year. She was gorgeous, funny, kind, and exactly what they all needed, especially him.

James didn't care what it took, but he was going to find a way to make his marriage with Cara real in every sense of the word. He wanted to love her and be the husband that she deserved.

CHAPTER SIX

The next couple of weeks passed. The dynamics of Cara and James' relationship shifted.

After the picnic, James started to show Cara affection. It was little things, like his hand brushing the top of hers when she passed him the potatoes at dinner, letting his hand rest on her back as he guided her through a door, or when he squeezed her hand during prayers at meals and at nights before bedtime.

James was still sleeping in Thomas' room, which she assumed was because neither of them were comfortable enough to broach the subject of him moving into the bedroom with her. She hoped in the near future that would change, and perhaps, they would become husband and wife fully.

Wanting to move their relationship in that direction, Cara asked James to go for a walk with her after they put the children to bed.

He slipped on his belt and put his pistol into its holster, causing Cara to question why.

"Where we live is rural," he explained. "We get coyotes often, and even wolves on occasion. It's not safe without some protection. Which reminds me, I need to take you out shooting sometime."

"Is that really necessary?" Cara asked with apprehension at the thought of it. "I've never even held a gun, let alone shot one."

"I think it is. Indians can sometimes still be found around these parts, along with all the wild animals. You should know how to protect yourself and the children if I'm not nearby to do it."

"Is it scary, to fire a gun?"

"The sound can be jarring the first few times you do it, but it gets easier and you get used to the noise."

She nodded, accepting she was still learning the rural life of the frontier. "If you think it best, then I trust your judgment."

"I'll carve some time out this week for us to go

out and do it," James said, holding the door open for Cara and letting his hand rest on her back, as she moved through, the touch making her happy.

The cool night air greeted them. It was a welcome relief from the long, hot summer days that had stretched out over the past month.

The air tickled Cara's skin, causing a shiver to crawl up her spine. She crossed her arms, rubbing them to make it stop.

James must have noticed because he reached out and put his arm around her shoulders. "Should we go in and grab you a shawl?"

She shook her head. "I much prefer your arm."

"Then I shall leave it right where it is," James said, pulling her in a little closer.

As they moved along the paths of the farm, James pointed out the different crops he was growing, as well as the perimeters of the property. He explained how he bought the first twenty acres with the money he saved up from the Army, how he used part of the profits to buy the next ten, and so on until he had a hundred-acre farm.

"You've really done an outstanding job. You should be proud of all you have accomplished."

"I am, but my biggest accomplishments are my three children. I love them dearly."

"And your first wife," Cara added, hesitantly. She took in a deep breath and waited for him to respond.

"I did, and part of me will always love Laura. Not only was she a good woman, but she was a kind and loving wife and mother."

"Do you think you could ever make room in your heart for another woman?" Cara asked, surprising herself, as much as James—whose eyes widened—with the question.

James didn't answer right away, and Cara was about to change the subject due to embarrassment, when he finally responded. "I want to be able to, Cara. I'm doing my best to find a way to make that happen."

It wasn't exactly the answer she wanted, but it was at least honest.

They walked in silence for several minutes before James finally said, "I'm glad you asked me to do this."

"Well, I had two reasons; I wanted to walk the farm and find out where the property lines are. I've been out to the barn and of course, the garden I take care of, but I haven't seen much else of the farm."

"What's the other reason?" James inquired,

stopping for a moment and turning to face Cara.

She took in a deep breath, pressing her lips together. Her eyes moved up to meet his and she whispered with a small hitch in her voice, "I wanted some time alone with you."

He wrapped his arms around her waist, saying, "Can't say I mind that. I like the idea of having a few uninterrupted moments with you."

"We don't get many with three children running around," Cara agreed, letting her body lean into his firm frame.

His mouth drifted down towards hers, hovering just inches away. For the briefest moment, she was certain he was going to kiss her. Before their lips could touch, a scream pierced the night's air.

"That's Becky," Cara blurted out in alarm.

Picking up the edge of her skirt, Cara took off towards the house, not thinking about anything other than getting to her daughter. Becky was always the quiet one, never causing any troubles. If she was screaming, something had to be terribly wrong.

Cara burst into the house and headed straight to the girls' room. Susan was sitting on the edge of the bed, patting Becky's back, who was hunched over with her knees tucked up against her chest.

"It's okay, Becky, please don't cry. Tell me what you need, and I'll get it."

"I want Ma," the little girl cried.

Cara hesitated. Though she viewed the children as her own now, she didn't know yet if it was reciprocated. She didn't want to make the situation worse, but her gut told her to go to the child.

Sitting down on the other side of her, Cara reached out and pulled the girl into her arms. "It's okay, Becky. I'm here," she affirmed, gently resting her chin against the girl's head. "Everything is going to be all right."

The girl let out a soft sigh, hiccupped a couple of times, then whispered, "I was so scared, Ma. I couldn't find you in my dream, I thought something bad happened to you, like a monster had swallowed you up whole."

"Nothing is going to take me away from you, Becky. I'm going to be with you for the rest of my life," Cara promised, her heart still warm from the sound of the girl referring to her as her mother.

"I want to be rocked back to sleep," Becky said, her eyes still fluttering as Cara stared down at her face.

"I can do it," Susan offered.

"No, I want Ma to do it," Becky insisted. "She'll keep the monsters away."

"What's going on? What happened?" Thomas said from the door, rubbing his eyes. "I thought I heard someone scream."

"It's okay now, Thomas. You can go back to bed," James stated, putting his hand on the boy's shoulder.

Thomas looked over at his sister and shook his head. "She said there's monsters. I want Ma, too."

The small boy rushed over and curled up on the other side of Cara, placing his head in her lap.

"Children, you shouldn't be an imposition to her like this," James protested.

"It's not an imposition," Cara gently corrected. "It's what a mother does. You can both sleep with me tonight," Cara said with a smile. "It will be fun to have a little company for once. Why don't the both of you head into my room and I'll be right there."

Susan came up and placed her hand on Cara's arm. "Maybe it would be a good idea if I stayed with all of you too, just in case you need some help with them."

"It's not necessary," Cara stated, but seeing the

girl's face wrinkle up in a fearful look, she added, "But it couldn't hurt."

Susan's face immediately brightened and she took off for the other room, leaving Cara alone with James once more.

"It's sweet of you to let them sleep with you. I have to say, I'm a bit disappointed this interrupted our night together."

"We'll have plenty more," she said, reaching out to touch the side of his cheek, enjoying the feel of his sun-kissed skin against her fingertips. "I promise."

As Cara slipped past her husband, their eyes locked for a moment and she saw something flicker in his eyes she would have sworn was desire. As quick it was there though, it disappeared, leaving her to wonder what would have happened if Becky hadn't had a nightmare. Would they have kissed? If they did, would it have led to more? Cara realized, she wanted her husband in every way possible, a tantalizing thought that carried her off to sleep.

———

Over the next few days, all James could think about was how he almost kissed Cara. In that moment, it was as if a floodgate opened and all the emotions he had been holding back came flooding into his heart.

He wanted his wife; he wanted her in every way a man could want a woman, but time was not on his side. The remaining crops were at a crucial time in their preparation for harvest. On top of having to plow the section of the farm that had already been harvested, he did not want weeds to grow in it, or risk their spread. Additionally, two of the pigs were due to have babies any day now, and Thomas had caught a cold and Cara was tending to him. The couple had no time to be alone together. The only option James had was to wait and bide his time until he could make his move and show his newfound desire for his wife.

James turned the corner of the field to head up the other direction, when suddenly the plow got stuck. The oxen groaned in complaint as James used the reins to try to push them forward. When it wouldn't work, James went to the back where the blades were and examined the area. A huge clump of hard dirt was wedged between two of the side blades. He pulled on it, but the obstacle wouldn't come free. Some of the dirt came off, revealing it was a rock.

Knowing his strength alone wouldn't do it, James looked for something he could use to leverage the rock. A large stick under a tree by the dirt road caught his eye. That should do the trick.

He quickly ran over and picked it up, then came back to the plow. He pushed one end under the rock, then slowly pushed down on the other. For a moment, he thought it was going to splinter and break off, but luck was on his side. The rock flew free, but so fast and without warning, it smacked James straight in the face, knocking him backwards.

James heard the oxen grunt and start to move, and he rolled to get away, knowing if he was too close his body would meet the end of the blades. Many farmers had died that way, and he didn't want to be the next. He wasn't quick enough though, and he felt the piercing pain of something digging into the flesh of his arm.

His scream pierced the afternoon air, causing the oxen to take off even faster than they were already going. He looked down at his arm and saw gushing blood flow out of a deep laceration. It was obvious he needed to wrap the wound, prompting him to yank off his outer shirt and tie it securely around his forearm.

With his good arm, James rolled over and pushed

off the ground, climbing to his feet. He stumbled towards the house, grateful that at least he was in the closest field and didn't have to make it very far.

James stumbled into the living room, calling out for Cara. "I need you!"

Cara rushed from the back part of the house and came to his side. Looking at his blood-soaked wrapped arm, she cried out, "What happened?"

"A plowing blade went over my arm. I'm going to need you to stitch it up."

Cara helped him over to the sofa, then knelt down beside him. "I don't know what I need to do that. You'll need to tell me."

James looked at her ashen face and felt awful that he put the worry in her eyes he saw there. He pushed the guilt aside and said, "Over in the drawer next to the sink, there's a needle and thread along with cloth for a bandage. You'll need to sterilize the wound and needle with alcohol."

With a nod, Cara went and got the needed supplies. A few minutes later, she returned and knelt down next to him again.

"I'm just glad the children are in the back playing. I wouldn't want them to see you like this," Cara said as tears formed in the corner of her eyes. She unwrapped the wound and gasped, "There's so much blood."

"It's not as bad as it looks," James encouraged. "I was lucky that the blade simply grazed me."

"What you're telling me is that it could have been much, much worse," Cara paused from threading the needle, glaring at him.

He tilted his head and crumpled his brows in pain, then realized she was mad at him because she cared what happened to him. "You needn't worry about me. Nothing like this has ever happened before."

"It only takes one time," she said, cleaning the needle with whiskey, then pressing her lips together, she reached out and pulled off the dirty shirt. "This is going to hurt."

Without a word, James nodded, then braced himself for the pain he knew was coming. True as rain, a searing shot of agony bolted up his arm where she poured the alcohol. He forced himself not to react, gritting his teeth together and closing his eyes, knowing that next the stitching was coming. It wasn't that he had a problem seeing blood; he'd seen his fair share during his time in the Army. Rather, what he didn't want to see was the mix of worry and anger in Cara's eyes for a moment longer.

Several minutes later, the stitching stopped, and Cara said, "I'm all done."

James opened his eyes and looked down at her work. "You did a great job."

"It was easier than butchering a pig, I'll give you that," she retorted, standing up and heading to the kitchen to put away the supplies. "This shirt is a loss now. I'll cut it up for rags, but we'll have to replace it next time we go to town."

"It was that or let myself bleed out. I figured it would be easier for you to replace my shirt rather than me," he said with a chuckle.

Cara came to sit down next to him. "That's not funny. You need to be more careful. The children have already lost one parent. They need you."

"Only the children?" James asked with a raised eyebrow, pulling himself up into a seated position.

Cara's cheeks tinged pink and her head dropped down, causing her to look at the ground. "No, not just them, me, too."

James reached out and placed his hand under her chin, lifting her face up so their eyes could meet.

"I'm glad you care what happens to me," he whispered, leaning towards her, his heart beating excitedly at their close proximity. The smell of Cara's new lavender perfume tickled his nose, making him giddy from the intoxicating scent.

As he looked at her, he couldn't help but notice how beautiful she looked with her red curls dangling in her face and her hazel eyes glistening with unshed tears. Her full lips were slightly parted, beckoning to be kissed.

Without waiting another moment, James reached out and placed his mouth upon hers. Instantly, heat radiated from the spot where their bodies connected, causing James to deepen the kiss. He reached out with his good arm and placed it at the back of her neck, letting his fingers tangle in her curls, the silky smoothness feeling wonderful against his skin.

"I wish it didn't take you nearly dying for us to do that," Cara stammered out breathlessly, pulling back to look him in the eyes. "Let's make sure the next time we kiss, it's under better circumstances."

"You have my word," he whispered, leaning forward to kiss her again, right before the children came bursting into the room demanding to know what was for lunch.

CHAPTER SEVEN

As James' arm healed, Cara and the children helped take care of many of his chores, along with a worker they temporarily hired to help with the heavier duties on the farm. They fell into a rhythm, each doing their best to help where they could.

It was on the following Saturday morning that something unexpected happened, creating bedlam in the home.

Susan came running out of her room, yelling in a scared voice. "I'm bleeding, I'm bleeding. I think I'm going to die."

Tears were streaming down the girl's face and she was shaking with fright.

Cara rushed to her side and started to inspect

her eldest daughter's body. When she found no visible wounds, she asked, "What are you talking about?"

"I was getting ready for the day, when I found blood in my..." she glanced around, and then whispered in Cara's ear so no one else could hear, "intimates."

Susan started to gulp big puffs of air, her face turning red with the hysteria. "Am...I going to...die like...Ma?" she managed to get out, before another bout of sobs took over.

Cara's eyes grew round with surprise, realizing that Susan was becoming a woman. What's more, she must have never discussed the matter with her mother before she passed away, which left the task to Cara.

"Is Susan dying?" Thomas shouted, running into the room. "I don't want someone else in the family to die, even Susan."

Becky followed right behind Thomas, putting her hand on the edge of Cara's blue dress and started bawling. "Not Susan, too. I don't want my sister to die like Ma did!"

"Children, that's enough, Susan isn't going to die," Cara shouted with exasperation.

All three Cassidy kids' eyes went wide as they

instantly stopped whatever they were doing. None of them had ever heard Cara shout, so it had a quieting effect unlike anything else.

"Becky and Thomas, I want you both to go outside and play while I talk to your sister." Turning to Susan, she wrapped her arms around the girl's shoulder, adding, "I think we need to have a private conversation."

A half hour later, Susan understood where babies came from and why she was bleeding. Cara explained how Susan would need to handle the situation each month, and that it wasn't something to be ashamed of, yet it was to be handled as discreetly as possible.

"Thank you, Ma. I don't know what I would have done if you weren't around," Susan said, reaching out and hugging Cara. "There's no way Pa would have known what to do."

"It must be one of the reasons God brought me to you when He did," Cara said with a smile. "Do you need me to explain anything else?"

She shook her head. "I don't feel so good. My tummy hurts. Can I go lay down?"

"Of course, you can, darling. Don't worry about helping with lunch. I can have Becky do it instead. It's about time she starts to learn the basics of cooking anyway. If the pain gets worse, let me know and I can get you a warm rag to wrap around your stomach."

Cara watched as Susan took off down the hall, much calmer than when she came from there earlier in the morning.

With a little time to spare before cooking the midday meal, Cara pulled out the sewing kit and set about patching the holes in Thomas' pants and Becky's stockings.

James came busting into the house, glancing around with a frantic look on his face. "Where is she? What happened?"

Cara stopped what she was doing and looked up. "Are you talking about Susan? She's fine," she stated dismissively, then started back to work on the patches.

"You're certain? Do we need to take her to the doctor? Thomas said she was frantically talking about bleeding."

Cara set down the clothes in her hand as she let out a sigh. It seemed this conversation was going to be longer than Cara had anticipated.

"I don't want you to be concerned about this, but Susan has reached that stage in life when every girl becomes a woman."

James' face creased up in confusion, and Cara realized she would have to explain further.

"She's started her monthly bleed," Cara stated bluntly.

This time, James's expression shifted to one of dismay, followed by aversion, and finally into one of acceptance.

"How is she doing with it?"

"She handled the information well and is resting."

James took a seat across from Cara at the table and ran his fingers through his brown hair, leaning back in his chair. "I don't know if I've ever been so frightened as I was when Thomas said Susan was hurt. I'm so glad it wasn't something life-threatening."

"There's nothing worse than losing a child. My mother was heartbroken when she lost my baby sister to the pox when I was but a young girl myself. I hardly remember my sister's face, but I can vividly remember my mother's pain the day my sister died."

"I'm sorry for your loss. Disease can be a cruel master. I know firsthand since Laura was taken by influenza. We thought it but a cold until it turned into something worse. By then, it was too late, and the doctor couldn't save her. I regret every day I didn't make her go into town sooner."

"It's not your fault, you know," Cara said, reaching out her hand and placing it on his chest. "You couldn't have known."

"My head knows that, but I still can't manage to let go of the guilt. It's why I reacted the way I did to the news about Susan. I didn't want to make a mistake by not taking whatever happens serious." Putting his own hand over hers, he added, "Thank you, by the way, for helping Susan with all of this. If you hadn't been here, I don't know what I would've done."

"Susan said the same thing," Cara stated with a chuckle. "It seems there's some things only a mother can handle."

"At least you don't have to worry about the 'becoming a man' conversation with Thomas. I promise to take that one."

Cara nodded. "I'll hold you to it."

"I need to get back to work," James said, standing up. "I was just coming in for a drink of water. I'll be back for the midday meal. Oh, and why don't I teach you how to shoot tomorrow. I have some time in the afternoon. I'm sure Thomas will want to come along too."

James leaned down and placed a quick peck on Cara's lips. The kiss was short but sweet, making her want more, but she knew it wasn't the time or place. She hoped sometime soon though, she would finally be able to get the alone time they both needed.

———

James decided it was time to claim his wife, and by extension, his bedroom once again. He had waited long enough, and the passion between them had swelled to a point where he knew they needed to be together.

The day before, when they had gone shooting, he could barely contain himself when he stood behind her and helped her aim the pistol. If Thomas hadn't been with them, their outing would have had a very different ending than just Cara learning how to hit a target.

Today was a new day and James had resolved he would wait no longer; however, he wanted to make their first time special. He decided that taking Cara somewhere private would be just the answer. Packing a few provisions for the outing, James decided he would take his wife to his favorite place.

"Where are we going?" Cara asked, letting James take her hand as he guided her out of the house.

"It's a surprise," he whispered against her ear. "I don't want to ruin it."

Cara let out a small giggle as she rolled her neck away. "That tickles."

James liked the way her laugh sounded to his ears—like little bells tinkling in the wind. It was all he could do to not swing her up into his arms, carry her back into the house, and into the bedroom. He had to remind himself the children were awake and that wouldn't be appropriate.

Instead, he led her along the stream until it reached the spot where it joined the main river at the edge of his property. At this exact spot, it formed a large circular hole that the family used for swimming. It was surrounded by trees, giving it natural shade, and there was a wooden swing hanging from one.

"This is beautiful," Cara stated with awe, as her eyes moved around the area. "I've never seen anything like it. You own it?"

"I don't know if anyone actually owns something this pristine, but it does exist on our property."

"Our property," she whispered. "I never thought of it that way."

"You should. We're husband and wife, and everything I have and will have is as much yours as it is mine." James reached out and took her face in his hands. "Including my heart, Cara; you have my heart now."

He could feel her body quiver where his hands touched her. She was breathing heavy, causing her lips to part, calling him to kiss her once again.

His mouth came down passionately, his lips taking hers for his own. He wrapped his arms around her waist, pulling her firmly against himself.

Her hands moved up his body, then curled around his neck, and she sighed in contentment.

James thought about putting her on the ground and taking her right there, but he didn't want to rush this. He knew it would be her first time, and he didn't want it to be like that.

With hesitancy, he pulled back from his enticing wife. "I could do that all day, but I think we should eat and take a swim first."

They both sat on the green grass, ready to enjoy the food James brought with them. He pulled out the sandwiches he made, along with two peaches, a small sack of mixed nuts, and a container of water.

"You thought of everything," Cara said with approval, accepting the sandwich he handed her.

"I want today to be special," he explained. "Part of that is me doing everything for you."

They ate their meal, talking about the children, the crops, and going into town for monthly provisions later in the week. By the time they finished, the sun was setting and both were contently full.

James suggested it was time for a swim. He started to undress, taking off his shirt first followed by his boots and pants, stopping at his undergarments. When Cara didn't do the same, he asked, "Do you plan to swim in your dress?"

Cara's face flushed red as she looked away. "No, but I've never undressed in front of a man."

"I'm not just any man, I'm your husband," James countered. "You don't have to be shy around me."

"Still, I would prefer if you turned around while I do it," she requested.

James didn't like her condition she put on their swimming time. He reminded himself that they were still a newly-wedded couple, one that hadn't consummated their marriage yet and as such, it was normal for her to feel the way she did.

Reluctantly, he turned around to give Cara her

privacy. A few moments later, he saw the blur of her running past him and jumping into the water.

His brows raised up in surprise as he rushed towards the water and joined her.

"You tricked me," he said with a chuckle, coming up beside her in the water. "I didn't expect you to rush in without me like that."

"I won't apologize that I'm modest."

"I wouldn't want you to be any way other than how you are. You bring so much joy to my heart," James declared, pulling her towards him in the water. "You're even more beautiful with the beams of the setting sun flaming around your face like that."

"You look so different with your hair slicked back from the water. I can see every line, every detail of your handsome face," she said, tracing her finger along the edge of his cheek. "I didn't know I would end up having such a good-looking husband when I came out West. I count myself lucky that not only are you a good provider and a steadfast friend, but that you make my heart race with passion when you look at me."

These were the words James had wanted to hear for the past few weeks. Now that he had, he planned to do something about it.

His lips descended strong and firm, taking possession of Cara's mouth, branding both her body and her heart as his forever. He hadn't been expecting it, but his wife had taken his in exchange. They were connected forever now, bonded through a single kiss that made them know without a shadow of doubt, they were one.

Before the kiss could lead to more though, howls penetrated the night air, growing closer until James was unable to ignore them anymore. Disappointed they had to stop what they were doing, he gently guided his wife over to the edge of the swimming hole.

"We can't stay here much after dark. The night life comes out and it isn't safe. We can continue this at home if you would like though," James suggested, reaching out a hand to help her from the water.

She nodded. "I'd like that. I think you should move back into your room with me. You've been sleeping in Thomas' room far too long."

They both put on their outer clothes, the awkwardness of changing in front of each other no longer an issue. Just as they were about to head towards the house, a low, deep growl behind them made them both freeze where they stood.

Slowly, they turned around to find a black wolf glaring at them. It was crouched forward on its front legs, as if preparing to pounce. Out of the shadows, two more wolves appeared next to the first one.

One wolf wouldn't be a huge problem, but a pack of them was a different story. If James and Cara were going to survive, they had to act fast.

James let his hand inch down his side until his hand was on the hilt of his left pistol.

"Do you remember what I taught you yesterday about shooting?" James inquired in a whisper.

"I do," she replied quietly.

"Then when I say so, you're going to reach for my pistol and we're going to draw both my guns at the same time. I'll take the two on the left, you take the one on the right. We have to be precise. You understand?"

Cara slowly nodded but didn't say another word.

James hoped she was prepared and didn't freeze up. He could try to pull both pistols and shoot all three, but if he missed or wasn't quick enough, one could lunge at them before he had a chance to stop them all. It was better to divide the work between Cara and him.

"Get ready, now," James commanded, pulling his own pistol from his holster while he felt Cara reach for the other. He aimed and fired at the first wolf, hitting his mark, then shifted his aim towards the other, doing the same. He also heard Cara fire the other pistol beside him. His first wolf hit the ground just as Cara's did too. His second wolf, however, did not. His shot must have missed the target because the animal attacked, running full steam at him. He put his arms up in defense, ready for the tearing of flesh that was sure to come. Before the wolf could reach its target though, a fourth gunshot rang out, causing the wolf to stop, give a small whine, and fall to the ground like the others.

"Did you just do that? Did you just save my life?" James asked, swiveling to face Cara.

She nodded, her hand still shaking with the gun in her hand. "I saw that final wolf charging at you, and I reacted. I couldn't let anything happen to you."

Reaching out, James took the gun from her hand and placed it back in his holster along with the other. "Thank you. I thought I could handle two of them, but it seems you're the marksman in this family."

Tears started to fall down her cheeks as her body moved from having small tremors to full body shakes. James was certain she was going into shock from the whole ordeal.

It was clear, she was in no condition to walk home. James lifted Cara up into his arms and made his way home with her. A half hour later, they entered the house. He was grateful to find the children were asleep.

Cara was passed out in his arms, exhausted from what happened. James halfway wondered if he might very well do the same if he didn't put her down and get off his feet immediately. He made his way over to the sofa and gently laid her down.

She mumbled something about being cold, prompting him to take the blanket at the end of the sofa and drape it over her. James debated about moving her into the bedroom, but he couldn't muster the energy. Instead, he decided to leave her there and sleep in the chair next to her. If she woke in the night, he didn't want her to be alone.

Silently, he said a prayer, grateful that they were both safe and no harm had come to them while they were out. Within a few moments, he was drifting off to sleep, praying that when they woke, all would be well again.

CHAPTER EIGHT

C ara woke up, her whole-body sore from the previous night. It must have been from all the stress the incident with the wolves caused.

She opened her eyes and realized she wasn't in a bed, but rather the sofa in the living room. What was she doing here?

A quick glance to the side revealed James was sleeping in the chair beside her. He was scrunched down low in it, with his arms folded across his chest. Surely, he wasn't comfortable like that?

Wanting to rectify that, she slowly got up from the sofa and took the blanket that had covered her and placed it on James.

His eyes flickered open and settled on her face. "You're awake."

"I am. I think I'm the first one, so I should probably start breakfast."

"Why don't you wake Susan and have her do that. You must be still exhausted from last night. I know I am."

"I'm fine," Cara said, not wanting to admit that he was right in his assessment. She wanted to continue to do her work around the house without interruption.

"You know what, I'm feeling much better," James said, standing up from the chair. "Why don't I help you instead."

"You don't need to do that," Cara resisted, watching as James moved past her and into the kitchen.

"I want to. I think it would be enjoyable to cook together," he said, placing a pan on the stove and then picking up some eggs from the counter. He glanced from the pan to the eggs and back again. "What do I do first?"

"Here, let me show you," Cara said with a chuckle, coming over to join him. "If you don't do it right, you'll burn them."

Cara demonstrated how to cook the eggs in the butter, then allowed James to do the next batch. They followed that up by frying some ham.

The smell must have woken the children because within a few minutes, two voices were asking when they could eat, while a third was offering to help.

"That's enough everyone," Cara said, gesturing towards the table. "Why don't you all go sit down. Your father and I've got this under control."

The children did as they were told while Cara and James finished preparing the meal. They brought the food over, and they spent the next half hour eating and talking about the plans for the day.

Susan and Becky offered to clean up, giving Cara time to wash up. She headed to the bedroom where she used the wash basin to clean her face, then pulled out a fresh, blue skirt, white blouse, and brown velvet vest. She put on the outfit, then went about putting up her hair.

Cara was finishing placing the last of the pins, when she heard shouting from the other end of the house. She rushed from the room and sprinted down the hallway, worried that one of the children was hurt.

To her surprise, a stranger stood in the middle of their living room. He wore a pair of boots and hat with a long, brown coat. On the left corner of it, a shiny silver badge read "Sheriff" on it.

Cara's blood ran cold as she saw the man staring at her with a look of interest. She had completely forgotten what happened with the man on the train, but suddenly, she wondered if her whole world was about to come crashing down.

"All of this is a misunderstanding. My wife told me all about what happened," she heard James explain to the lawman.

"That might be, Mr. Cassidy, but the warrant came across my desk and I have to enforce it. She'll have her day in court where she can tell her side of it."

"That man is lying," James protested. "You can't take my wife away because one man decides to tell a bunch of lies."

"My hands are tied. There were witnesses." The sheriff shook his head and came over to Cara's side. "Mrs. Cassidy, I'm sorry to do this, but I have to take you in now. You're under arrest for the attempted robbery and assault of Jeremiah Butes."

The lawman reached out for her with a set of iron handcuffs and slipped them on her delicate wrists. The weight of them pulled on her shoulders, almost toppling her over.

Before he could escort her out though, Thomas

came running up, and pushed himself in between them. "You can't take our Ma," he screamed out in anger. "She's ours! We need her!"

Becky came up next, grabbing the edge of her skirt. "Don't go, Ma, please don't go," she whimpered, burying her face in Cara's skirt.

Cara could see Susan standing by her father, crying with her hands clenched in front of her. The situation seemed like one giant nightmare. All she wanted to do was go to her children and comfort them, but her hands were literally and figuratively tied.

"Mr. Cassidy, you need to help me with your children," the sheriff requested. "Let's not make this worse than it has to be."

"Susan, help me with them, please," James ordered, both of them coming up to do as the sheriff bided.

Susan easily scooped Becky into her arms, who continued to cry into her sister's shoulder, while the older girl continued to shed her own tears.

Thomas wasn't quite as easy to wrangle. "You're not taking my Ma. Not ever, ever," he said, pulling his leg back and kicking the sheriff's shin with his foot. "Let her go, right now!"

"That's enough, Thomas, you come with me right this instant," James demanded in a loud voice. He grabbed his son by the arm and pulled him away. "We're going to get your Ma back, but we can't do it this way. We have to obey the law."

The sheriff opened the door and guided her through the opening, the Cassidy family following behind. They stopped at the edge of the porch while the sheriff lifted her up into the wagon.

"I'm going to fix this, Cara, I promise," she heard James vow from behind her. "No matter what it takes, I'm going to make sure you're set free."

Cara wanted to believe her husband, but she knew firsthand how a person could be innocent and still end up on the wrong end of the noose. Her own father had it happen, and part of her feared the same would happen to her because of that fateful day on the train.

As they headed down the dirt road towards Mitchell, Cara wondered what was in store for her. Would she spend the rest of her life in prison? If that happened, how did they treat women in those places? Would they abuse her, starve her, or worse? There was always the option that she might end up dead. Did they hang women in these parts? She wasn't sure, but it was the wild West. Anything was possible.

Tears slipped down her cheeks as despair took root in her heart. Just a couple of hours ago, her life made sense. She was happy with children she loved, a home she finally could manage, and a husband that she was beginning to care for. Now, it was all gone, and she was facing a life without any of it, a life not worth living even if she managed to stay alive.

When they entered the jail, both deputies sat up in their chairs behind their desks, and looked over at Cara and the sheriff. They didn't seem surprised by her presence as much as uncomfortable, and she realized they probably didn't have many women arrested in the area.

"I was able to secure you a separate cell, Mrs. Cassidy, but you should know, there's other lawbreakers in the one next to you. They'll try to get you to engage with them but avoid talking to them at all costs. They're in here for very bad crimes."

Cara didn't argue the point that according to what she was arrested for, she was in there for attempted murder, which was most likely equal or worse than anything the men in the jail had done.

She was already embarrassed about the false accusation and what everyone must think of her because of it. She didn't want to draw more attention to what put her there.

The sheriff placed her in the jail cell, explained there was a small cot in the corner, and that if she needed to use the privy, she could ask, and someone would take her to the outhouse behind the sheriff's office.

Not sure what to do once she was left alone in the cell, she glanced around trying to figure it out.

"Hey there, lassie, you're from Ireland, aren't you?" she heard a man ask with an Irish accent. "We might be kin, you and me. We should put our heads together and think of a way to get out of here."

Cara looked over at the man next to her, separated only by thin metal bars, leering at her in a way that made her skin crawl with disgust.

Trying to do what the sheriff suggested, she ignored the balding brown-haired man.

She decided she would sit on the cot which was in the furthest corner of the cell. With any luck, she could hide in the shadows and pass the time unnoticed until she figured out what to do next.

"Listen here, lassie, you shouldn't ignore your

elders. It's quite rude," the man snarled. "Didn't your parents teach you better than that? I guess not, considering you're in here," he said, with a heckling laugh.

Cara's head whipped to the side, her eyes narrowing in anger as she yelled, "Don't talk about my parents like that. You don't know anything about them."

"Leave her alone," a second man growled out from the shadows. "That lady doesn't need your sort harassing her."

The other man came towards the bars. He towered over the shorter Irish man as he glared at him, intimidating him enough to force him to move out of the way.

The tall, dark-haired man leaned against the bars, his hands curling around them as he said in a softer voice. "Sorry about him. He shouldn't have bothered you, and I'll make sure he doesn't again." Looking her up and down, he inquired, "What are you in for? I can tell by your proper clothes and lack of rouge, you're not a harlot. I can't imagine what a dignified woman could do to end up in here."

"I was accused of robbery and assault if you must know, but I didn't do it," she stated with a huff, crossing her arms. "Though the sheriff doesn't seem to care about my innocence."

"That's not his job, despite what the badge infers. He's simply here to carry out orders, like most of the sheep that are the cogs in the wheel of this world. It's a false sense of security really, believing that any of us are safe when there are so many, truly, evil people in this world. Everyone needs a good protector against it, and I'm quite good at protecting a damsel in distress." His words sounded like poison disguised as honey. She suspected the serpent in the Garden of Eden couldn't have sounded more alluring.

"I don't know how much protecting you can do," she countered with disbelief, "like the rest of us, you're in here. Besides, my husband will be by shortly to sort this whole mess out."

The man rebuffed her declaration. "Is that so? I doubt a good, upstanding citizen like James Cassidy will want to keep his mail order wife now that the truth's come out about what she's accused of doing."

"How do you know my husband?" Cara asked, mystified.

"I know some people who were on the train with you. I've heard the details about what happened. I could use a girl with your skills, so my offer of protection comes along with a proposal of a job. Once I get out of here, and I will be getting out of here since I've got friends in high places, I can work on getting you out too. Then, together, we can make a lot of money. There are more pockets of unsuspecting travelers than you could ever imagine out here in the West. I could train you so you would never get caught again."

"You're mistaken, I'm not that type of woman," Cara defended herself, angry that this man who didn't even know her, assumed she was guilty just like everyone else did. Not only that, but that she would want to commit herself to a life of crime.

Angry at the entire situation, Cara laid down on the cot and turned to face the wall. She didn't want to talk to anyone else in this place.

Did that mean that her husband would believe all the lies too? Was he going to leave her here to rot? Part of her wouldn't blame him since they'd only been married a couple of months and he had his children to think about. Did he want to subject them to what was to come in defending her? If by some miracle, she was to be freed, would he want her soiled reputation to follow them the rest of their lives?

All the swirling questions in her head plagued her thoughts. She wanted to sleep, but it evaded her. What was she going to do? How was she going to survive this? Would she ever see her family again?

In silence, she sent up a prayer asking God to help her.

Just as she was starting to fall asleep, she heard a commotion behind her in the center of the room, along with several voices talking.

"I can't believe this old coot was able to fool so many unsuspecting families," one of the voices stated with shock. "Did you hear he did over a dozen weddings and nearly three dozen funerals?"

"Who cares who buries you, it's who marries you that matters. If your marriage isn't recognized by God, you're living in sin with your woman. I wouldn't want that hangin' over my head," the other man said.

"You have no idea what you're talking about. God appointed me to this task. I was just doing his bidding," said a third voice—one that was familiar enough to make Cara's heart skip a beat in dread.

Cara turned over and was shocked to see the man who married her to James. He was standing in handcuffs between the two deputies.

"Right, and I'm betting you want us to believe

God told you to steal the unsuspecting couples' wedding rings and fleece them for money when you had no business conducting religious ceremonies? You're not even an ordained minister," the first deputy stated with disgust. "You deserve every bit of justice coming your way."

"Should we put him in the cell with the two men, or do you think the sheriff would be mad if we put him in with the woman?" the second deputy asked the first one.

"He isn't coming in here with me," Cara shouted, jumping to her feet in anger. "I don't want that snake anywhere near me!"

"What's gotten into her?" the second deputy inquired, his eyes growing wide with shock.

"My guess, I think this faux preacher presided over her now known-to-be fake wedding," said the tall man from the other cell, coming over to watch the entertainment. "If you put him in there with her, I'm betting she's going to rip his eyes out for the disservice. Granted, I would love to see her get her hands on him, but I think your sheriff would frown upon letting that happen."

"Shut up, you. You probably just want him in there so you can toy with him like you do all the other reprobates that come and go. I can't wait until the marshal's office finally sends someone to pick you up."

"What can I say, I'm a big fish in a little pond here," the tall man said with a shrug. "The marshal wants to make sure I go to a big pond for my trial."

"Be quiet, we're tired of hearing you talk, Riker," the first deputy stated. "But we'll throw the preacher in with you. Be on your best behavior, now."

They put the imposter inside the cell, and then closed and locked it.

Cara stared at the man across from her, the man who she put her faith and trust into marrying her to her husband. She was shocked to find out he was a liar and a thief, and that her marriage was a sham because of his dishonesty.

"How could you do it?" Cara accused. "How could you lie to all those people, to me, to my family?"

"I'm sorry, do I know you," the fake preacher asked with confusion that seemed all too convenient.

"Don't pretend you don't know me. I deserve an answer as to why you did it," she spat out in anger. "You tricked me, along with a lot of other people, and you need to tell me why."

"I'm not sure what you're talking about," the imposter said with a shrug. "I've met a lot of people during my travels as a preacher, I can't be expected to remember every one of them. I'm going to go lay down now," the man said, turning around to head to one of the cots.

Riker, however, didn't let him get away. He grabbed the fake preacher by the neck and dragged him over to the bars, slamming his face against them.

"No one is buying your nonsense about not remembering," Riker growled out. "You're going to answer the lady, or I'm going to continue to push your face forward until it slides through these bars. Do I make myself clear?"

The imposter squealed out, "Yes, yes, just let me go."

Slowly, Riker released the fake preacher, but continued to stand right behind him only inches away. "Don't make me put my hands on you again. If I do, you won't like what happens next," the tall man threatened. "Now, answer her."

The fake preacher nodded, then swallowed several times before speaking. "Miss, it's a cutthroat world out here in the West. The first time I did it, I was starving. I heard someone needed a preacher. It wasn't a complete lie; I went to seminary. I just didn't finish, so I figured what could it hurt? They would be married, and I would eat. Then someone referred me to someone else, and before I knew it, I had a thriving business."

"You mean a thriving deception," she corrected with bitterness. "You're deplorable to prey on unsuspecting people with such an elaborate hoax. I hope you rot in jail for the rest of your life."

Without another word, the fake preacher slinked away, his head hanging low as he went over to the cot.

"Why did you do that? Why did you stand up for me?" Cara implored of Riker.

"I told you I'd protect you, and despite what it might appear, I'm a man of my word," Riker explained. "If your husband—or should I say the man who thinks he's your husband—doesn't come for you or changes his mind about being with you once he finds out the truth about your marriage, I want you to know you have another option."

Cara wasn't sure what to make of what Riker was saying and wondered if his predictions of the future were going to come through. He seemed to know the ways of the world, so was he right about James? Was her marriage—or whatever it was between them—over? Was all that was left for her a choice between a jail cell or a life on the run with a man like Riker?

As she lay curled up on the cot, filled with overwhelming despair, she tried to keep the tears at bay. It was no use, however; they gushed free from her eyes, trickling down her cheeks as she quietly cried herself to sleep.

———

As soon as James calmed the children down, he gathered them up with a few essentials and drove the wagon into Mitchell. He took the children over to the church where he asked the pastor and his wife to watch them while he tried to sort everything out.

His next stop was the post office where he wired a telegraph to his friend from the Army who had become a Pinkerton Agent. He wanted his friend to find out everything he could about Jeremiah Butes and where James could locate the wretched man. He was smart enough not to leave his wife's fate in the hands of overburdened lawmen with limited resources. It was up to James to save her.

James told the postmaster he would be back

later to check on a reply, and then headed over to
the jail. He needed to see his wife. He'd been so
busy planning out his next steps in what to do, he
hadn't let it really sink in there was a possibility he
might lose her. The idea of it scared him because
she had become essential not only to the children's
way of life, but his own. They needed Cara.

He entered the sheriff's office and headed over
to the first desk. A young blond-haired deputy sat
behind it with his boots up on the desk. When he
saw James, he quickly slung his legs down and
asked, "What can I do for you, sir?"

"I'm here to see my wife, Cara Cassidy," James
stated plainly.

The deputy's eyebrows raised in surprise and he
mumbled under his breath, "This should be inter-
esting," as he stood up and gestured for James to
follow him.

What did that mean? Why did the deputy seem
like he was expecting there to be a problem when
he talked to Cara?

"Miss, you have a visitor," the deputy said,
glancing over at James. "He says he's your
husband."

Cara rolled over and jumped to her feet,

rushing to the bars when she saw James outside them.

"You're here, you're here! I can't believe you came for me," she stammered out, wrapping her fingers around his on the bar.

James brows came together in a furrow, confused by her reaction. "Of course, I came. Why wouldn't I? You're my wife."

"Now, is she? I think you to should probably discuss that fact," said a tall dark-haired man, who came up to the bars of the cell next to Cara's.

"What's he talking about? Who are you?"

"I'm a friend of hers," the tall man said, shrugging towards Cara.

"I wouldn't go that far," Cara protested, giving a dirty look towards the other man. "But Riker is right; we do need to talk about our marriage."

"What about our marriage?" James asked, fear taking hold that she was going to tell him she didn't want to be married to him anymore. Had she taken up with this Riker fellow? Were the accusations true? He'd always thought she'd told him the truth about what happened, but was he a fool for believing her? Had he been blinded by his need for help and her alluring beauty? He didn't want to think so, and from what he knew of Cara, he would bet his life she was a good and decent woman.

Cara pressed her lips together as she glanced over at the other cell then back at James. "They just brought in another prisoner, one that you might recognize over in the other cell."

James leaned back and looked where she was talking about. To his surprise, laying on a cot was the preacher who married them.

"What on earth is the preacher doing here? Why is he in a jail cell?" James asked with incredulousness.

"It's complicated," Cara whispered.

"It's not that complicated," Riker countered with a shrug. "Just tell him the truth, the preacher is a fake, as is your marriage."

"What are you talking about? What's going on?" James asked, not wanting to accept what the other man just said.

"I hate to say it, Cara, but I think you've got a daft one on your hands. You should walk away like I've told you while you've got a chance."

"I think you should stay out of this, before I make you stay out of it. This is between my wife and me," James shouted in anger.

"What aren't you getting? She's not your wife," Riker stated slowly for affect.

"Is this true?" James asked, turning his attention to Cara, and ignoring Riker for the time being. "Is our marriage built on a deception?"

Cara nodded. "I just found out myself. Theodore Demont—if that's even his real name—is a liar and a crook. He's been preying on strangers all over the West, pretending to be a preacher. He's even stolen our rings and given us fake ones in exchange."

"I have to admit, switching them in a hollowed-out Bible is impressive," Riker stated with a perverse respect for the other criminal. "He might be a sniveling weasel, but he's smarter than I first gave him credit for."

"Can you just shut up?" James snapped at Riker. "I don't need your commentary about our lives."

Riker raised his hands and backed up. "I get it; you've got enough problems to handle. Good luck, you're going to need it."

"I understand if this changes your mind about helping me. We don't have to be together now," Cara said, her bottom lip trembling as tears formed in her eyes. "After finding this out, you can wash your hands of me knowing you don't owe me anything."

"That's not true," James declared, shaking his head. "I owe you everything, Cara. You've helped the children be happy again, you've helped me heal and shown me I can open my heart again, and you've renewed my faith in life again. I can't live without you. I won't. I stand by what I said earlier; I'm going to find a way to set you free."

He leaned between the bars and placed his lips on hers, but the deputy came up and tapped him on the shoulder. "You can't do that in here. It's not allowed."

Grudgingly, James stepped back, giving a final squeeze to his wife's hands. "I'll be back as soon as I can. Keep strong, Cara."

She nodded right before he turned around and headed back to the post office.

He waited there for the rest of the day before he finally got a response from his friend. What he received shocked him.

Jeremiah Butes is a dangerous man and well connected. Forwarding the information we have on him. Be careful.

. . .

Along with the short telegraph was a piece of paper with multiple arrest reports for Jeremiah Butes for assaulting young women. Though there was enough to arrest him, none of the charges stuck. James wondered why that was. Could it be due to the "connections" his friend alluded to? If that was the case, how would he ever be able to get Cara's charges dismissed?

Noticing there was a note stating that Mr. Butes was staying at a hotel in the nearby town of Yankton, James decided he would go there and see what he could dig up on the man. There had to be something he could do to help Cara.

James retrieved his horse from the livery and mounted him, then took off towards the other southern South Dakota town. He pushed his horse as hard as he could without harming the animal.

When he arrived in town, he tied his horse off at one of the hitching posts, then went to the hotel. Mr. Butes wasn't there. The hotel clerk mentioned that he often spent time over at the Long Rifle Saloon, prompting James to go there.

James entered the saloon and the smell of stale sweat and souring booze overwhelmed him. The place was dingy with decaying furniture as well as people. He resisted the urge to cover his nose with his hand, knowing it would raise eyebrows with the rowdy men in the establishment.

James moved around the room, trying to figure out if Jeremiah Butes was presently in the saloon. It would've helped if he knew what the man looked like, but he could only guess. He eliminated the men gambling at the two tables since one set was talking about local politics while the other was discussing the latest cattle drive. That left the men at the bar, and there were two of them.

He sat down next to the first one and watched him from the corner of his eye.

"What can I get you?" the barkeep asked, his hands resting on the wooden counter.

"I'll have a whiskey," James ordered, knowing he wouldn't drink it, but not ordering one would make him stand out in all the wrong ways.

The barkeep grunted, poured the drink, and slammed it down hard on the bar. James paid the barkeep the required amount, then waited to hear the man next to him speak. He hoped the other man would say something to let James know whether or not he was Butes.

They sat in silence for several minutes before the other man finished his drink. "Let me have another one," the man slurred out, sliding the glass across to the barkeep. "I want one more before I head upstairs to my room with that beauty over there," he said, shrugging towards a brunette saloon worker in the corner of the room.

Well, that ruled him out, considering he was staying at the saloon. That left just the other man at the end of the bar. James stood up, casually made his way down, and took a seat next to the final man.

Butes was hunched over the bar, his hands wrapped around a glass of a dark liquid. After a few moments, he must have noticed James because he asked, "What do you want?"

James weighed his response, deciding that in order to get the man's guard down, it would be better to keep it casual and let him drink a few more before he started questioning him about Cara and the train.

"Just wanting to have a drink, like everyone else in the place," James stated, lifting his drink up to his lips for effect.

"Mighty odd of you to come on down next to me when you were perfectly good at the other end."

"He wasn't the best company," James explained. "I'd rather have someone to talk to that can hold a conversation as well as his liquor."

"Then I'm your man. I can do both," Butes

stated before chugging the last of his drink to prove the point. "As long as you're buying."

James would rather chew nails than buy this man a drink, but he needed to get him comfortable enough that he'd start talking about what happened with Cara. A confession was the only way James would be able to clear his wife's name, and it needed to be public.

"Certainly," James confirmed, nodding towards the barkeep. "Give the man whatever he likes, it's on me."

"I'll take another bourbon," then looking over at James, he added, "Thanks."

"You're welcome," James said with a nod. "I figure you can tell me what's what around here, so it's the least I can do."

"What do you want to know?" Butes inquired.

James knew better than to get to the core of what he wanted to discuss, so he started off with a neutral topic.

"Is there a lot of work here in Yanktown?"

"If you're looking, you can find something to do. Some of its reputable, some of it's not. You can always find a way to make a quick dollar around here if you're so inclined."

"What about the women? Are there a lot of pretty women around here?"

"Not as many as most of us would like. Women are less common out here in the West, but there's always a bar wench to be had here in the saloon." Butes leaned towards James and whispered, "Can't vouch for the quality or the looks, but they can keep you content sure enough."

James pretended to look around at the women working in the saloon. He shrugged. "I can see what you mean. Not a lot of options—no fair-haired or red-headed women," James said, hoping to bait the other man.

"I know, I know, I keep telling the barkeep to get better merchandise, but it's slim-pickings out here," Bute stated with a sigh. "Not like back East where a man could get any number of young women. I tell you, when I was back there, I was knee-deep in every kind you could imagine. My favorites were redheads though. I can't resist getting a taste of them."

James had to bite back the bile that rose in his throat at how crudely the man was talking about women, as if they were no more than a commodity to take advantage of.

Trying to focus on getting the answers he

needed instead of the anger he felt, James inquired, "Was there ever one that got away? One you wished you could have gotten but didn't?"

"That doesn't happen to me too often. When I want something, I get it, no matter what it takes. It's actually why I'm out here. I chased a little redheaded filly all the way from Massachusetts out here to South Dakota. As luck would have it, she got away before I could get what I wanted from her."

"And what was that?" James asked, forcing himself to hide his anger, knowing he would hate the answer.

"Every inch of her. I mean, I had her mother. She fought me the whole time, but in the end, I got what I wanted. Didn't mean to end up hurting her, but the husband got the blame and the noose. I was free to find my opportunity to get ahold of the daughter. I figured if the mother was good, the daughter would be even better."

It was all James could do to restrain himself from lunging at the man and choking the life out of him. It was bad enough that he had attacked Cara and was lying about her robbing him. As it turns out, he was responsible for what happened to Cara's parents and how she ended up alone.

"What's keeping you around here then?" James asked, wanting to understand the whole picture.

"I'm just saving up my money until I can get back home. That, and I want to wait to make sure the redhead pays for making a fool of me. No one pulls one over on Jeremiah Butes and gets away with it."

This time, James couldn't control the growl that came out. He reached out and grabbed the other man by the shirt collar. He yanked the creep towards him, saying, "Jeremiah Butes, let me introduce myself. James Cassidy."

The other man's eyes grew wide with first shock and then fear as he stammered out, "How... how did you find me?"

"You messed with the wrong redhead," James stated with rage. "My wife."

"I think you're mistaken—"

"No, there's no mistake about what you just said. You made it clear and I'm going to make this clear, you're going to pay for what you did to Cara and her family. First, you're going to confess to what you did, and then if you're lucky, you'll spend the rest of your rotten life in prison."

Butes ripped free from James' grasp, his eyes

narrowing into slits. "You can't make me do anything. I'm going to walk right out of here."

When he tried to move past James, he blocked Butes' path. His hand went to the hilt of his pistol, remembering his friend warned him that Butes was dangerous.

Butes' eyes flickered towards the door, then to James and where his hand rested. He placed his own hand on the hilt of his gun, making it obvious he would fight to get away.

"Gentleman, we don't want any trouble in here. You best be taking this outside," the barkeep suggested, gesturing towards the door.

"We can't go outside. I need witnesses for this," James explained. "This man just confessed to being responsible for my wife's mother's murder, her father's hanging, and attacking my wife. He also framed her for a crime she didn't commit simply because she was unwilling to let him have his way with her. Because of these crimes, I'm detaining Mr. Butes until the local sheriff can come and arrest him."

"You're going to try to do this?" Butes asked with incredulousness. "I should warn you, I'm an expert shot. You don't want to tangle with me."

"And I should tell you, I'll give my last breath to

save my wife," James vowed. "You can draw on me, but I won't let you leave here."

"We'll see about that," Butes declared, pulling his gun from its holster.

James instinctively pulled out his own gun, then dove out of the way behind a nearby table. A spray of bullets came flying at him, causing James to wait until there was a pause in the firing. He looked over the table and saw Butes making a run for the door.

He debated about shooting Butes, but if he killed him, there was no way his wife would get exonerated. James needed him alive to confess to what he did.

James stood up from behind the table and took off after Butes, putting his gun back in the holster before exiting the saloon. Just as they reached the outside, James tackled the other man, knocking his gun out of his hands. He tried to restrain Butes, but he was rolling around trying to get free from James' grasp.

Butes managed to get on his back and swung his fist up, connecting with James' jaw. The impact made James see stars, but he pushed the pain away focusing on stopping Butes from escaping.

They wrestled on the ground for several seconds before James was finally able to subdue the other man. He stood up, pulling the other man up behind him.

"I'm taking you to the sheriff's office," James stated firmly. "Don't make this more difficult than it has to be."

A growing crowd of men from the saloon was forming around James and Butes, all of them trying to get a peek at what was going on.

"I'm not going to jail! I'd rather die," Butes screamed, slamming his head forward and hitting James in the center of his forehead.

James stumbled back, grabbing his head with one hand and reaching for his gun with the other. He tried to focus on Butes, wanting to make sure he hadn't found his gun on the ground. The last thing he needed was to get in another fire fight with his eyesight still blurry.

James raised his gun up and leveled it at the other man, yelling, "Don't make me shoot you, but no matter what happens, you're coming with me."

"Never," he hollered back, diving for his gun.

Butes' hand wrapped around the gun. He lifted it up and aimed it at the crowd. Before James had a chance to react, gunfire rang out. James waited to feel the pain from the bullet ripping through his flesh, but it never came.

To his surprise, blood spread across the chest of Butes, causing James to scream, "No, I need him alive!"

Rushing to the man's side, James bent down beside him. "You can't die like this. I need you to clear Cara's name. Live! After all you did to her and her family, you owe her that."

The man started to choke, his eyes rolled back, and before James could do anything to stop it from happening, he was gone.

James looked over at the crowd, bewildered by what happened. Who shot him and why?

There was only one dark-haired man with a jagged scar on his cheek, holding a gun. He had a look of triumph on his face as he placed the pistol back in his holster. "That should have been done a long time ago. Butes was a rotten, no good, fool. The world is better off without him."

James stood up and came over to the crowd. "I'm not arguing with your assessment of the man, but I needed him alive to clear my wife's name. Now that he's dead, I have no idea how I'm going to save her from prison."

"We can help with that," the barkeep said, gesturing to the group of men around him. "I overheard your conversation with him this evening."

"And we've all heard him brag about his escapades, including the ones with your wife's family. We can tell the sheriff the truth and help free your wife," one of the men next to the barkeep explained.

"Thank you," James said with a nod. "It's time for me to go get my wife back."

CHAPTER NINE

When Cara saw James enter the jail with a smile on his face, hope filled her heart. His happy demeanor must mean that he had found a way to get her out of this place.

She rushed up to the bars and wrapped her hands around them. Once he arrived at her cell, he put his hands on hers.

"I have some good news. You're getting out of here today," James informed her.

"How did you manage that?"

"I tracked down Jeremiah Butes—the man who attacked you—and questioned him about what he did to you. He admitted it to me, with witnesses to hear. Before I could get him to the sheriff's office, he got violent, and was killed by a man at the saloon."

"He's dead? I don't know what to think about that," Cara confessed. "I mean, he nearly ruined my life, but I wouldn't wish anyone dead."

"Butes did it to himself. He had every opportunity to turn himself in peacefully, but he refused. He was going to kill me if that other man hadn't intervened. Besides, after everything I found out about what he's done, he didn't deserve to live." James brows furrowed together as he glanced away for a moment. After a couple of seconds, his eyes came back to meet hers and the look in his eyes made Cara realize there was more to the story.

"What aren't you telling me?"

James pressed his lips together, then let out a heavy sigh. "In the process of finding out the truth, Butes also admitted that he followed you from back East out here to South Dakota."

"What are you talking about? How is that possible? Did he notice me on the train?"

"No, his obsession with you went back much further than that. I'm sorry to tell you this, Cara, but he was the one responsible for killing your mother, and after she was gone, his focus shifted to you."

Cara couldn't believe what she was hearing. It was hard to accept that the same man who attacked her was the man who attacked and killed her mother. That means Butes was also responsible for her father's death since the town blamed him. They hanged him for her mother's death when it was never him to begin with. She had always known her father was innocent, but to hear the proof of it now, made her grateful that finally he was vindicated. She could now put her past in the past where it belonged.

"I don't want to think about Butes or what he did anymore. I just want to go home and see the children."

"The sheriff's processing your release right now. As soon as he's finished with the documents, we can head home, but we have to pick the children up at the church first. The pastor and his wife are watching them."

An hour later, they were loaded up in the wagon and headed to the church to get the children.

They entered the white, wooden building at the edge of town. The children were helping set out the supplies for service the next morning. When they saw Cara come through the doors, they squealed with delight and ran towards her.

"Ma, Ma, you're back," Thomas shouted as he ran up to her and threw his arms around her waist.

Becky came up next, placing her hand in Cara's. "We missed you so much, Ma. We were so worried we would never see you again."

"I wouldn't let that happen," Cara vowed. "I care about you children too much for that. Besides, your pa made sure of it too."

Susan was the final one to arrive. She hugged Cara, saying, "I was wrong. I can't do it all on my own. We need you, Ma."

Cara's heart warmed at the high praise. "Just so you know, I need you too," Cara whispered against her eldest daughter's ear. "Who else would teach me how to tend the garden?"

As they exited the church, Cara was grateful to be returning to the farm. In the back of her mind, however, she still worried about what they were going to do about their marriage, or rather, lack of one. They needed to decide what to do, and quickly before both their reputations were ruined for good.

———

Once they arrived home and fed the children, James asked Cara to join him in the living room.

"We need to talk about what happened with the preacher and what that means for this family," James started. "We can't be living together if we aren't married. It's unseemly."

"I agree," Cara said with a nod. "All the reasons we got married quickly the first time still exist. The question is, do we both still want to go through with it a second time? We haven't consummated the marriage, which means we can both walk away from this without any ramifications."

James tilted his head to the side as he looked at her. "Why are you asking that? Have you changed your mind about us, about staying here?"

Cara looked down at the ground, then whispered, "I thought I was amiable with the idea of being in a cordial marriage; one where I worked well with my husband to build a life together. I convinced myself I could live life like a business agreement, but I'm not sure of that anymore."

"What do you mean? What do you want then? Do you want to leave us?" James inquired, hoping that perhaps she wanted to have a real marriage as much as he did. Did he dare to hope that perhaps they both wanted the same thing?

She took in a deep breath, then said, "I want to love, and be loved in return. If that can't happen, if you won't let that happen, then I don't see how we can have a future. I would feel I had to leave—"

Before she finished, the children burst into the room.

"You have to stay married. You're our Ma," Thomas declared. "We can't go back to Susan's cooking."

"You can't leave us again," Becky said, her lip trembling as tears puddled in the corner of her eyes. "We just got you back."

"They're right you know. You can't leave. We love you," Susan stated firmly. "You don't leave people when you love them."

"Susan's right. If Pa says you have to go, then we will all go with you," Thomas declared.

"There's no need for that. I want her to stay too," James declared with a grin. "I don't want Cara to ever leave us again."

"Good, we don't want you to ever make her leave," Thomas said, crossing his arms over his chest as he narrowed his eyes at his father.

"Who said anything about making her leave?" James asked with incredulousness.

"We heard you ask about her leaving," Thomas explained. "We thought you changed your mind."

"No, that will never happen," James corrected. Turning his attention to Cara, he added, "I love you, Cara. I've known for a while now, but I was too afraid to tell you. You need to know it, and I need to say it. I love you so much that I can't imagine my life without you in it."

Happy tears streamed down Cara's cheeks. "I love you too, James." Then looking at all her children, she added, "Actually, I love all of you with all my heart."

"Now that we've got that settled, we need to figure out what to do about our wedding." James came up and placed his arms around her shoulders. "I already talked with the pastor in town and he said he could marry us tomorrow at the church if we're willing."

"I think that sounds like a marvelous plan," Cara stated with a smile.

"I guess that means one more night in the barn," James stated with a sigh. Then he leaned forward and whispered so only Cara could hear, "I can't wait to be back in my own bed with you tomorrow night."

"Me too," she whispered back. "Tomorrow night is going to be wonderful."

James turned to face Cara, then leaned down and placed his lips upon hers. The kiss was tender and sweet, a promise of the love and happiness to come.

CHAPTER TEN

The next day, Cara, James, and the children went back to Mitchell. James took Cara over to the dress shop and let her pick out a new dress for the wedding. There was a lovely white one made from satin and lace the shop owner suggested, but Cara was worried about the practicality of it. She wanted to be able to reuse it again for special occasions, and white wasn't the most forgiving of colors.

"You don't need to worry about that," James insisted. "The farm is doing great. I've saved up enough that we can expand the house and buy more land if we want."

"Then shouldn't we continue to save our money for that? I agree a new dress would be nice, and if I am to get one, why not settle on a pretty blue or yellow one that I can use often?"

"This is your chance to have the wedding you've always wanted, Cara. The first time, you got married in a dress covered in rips and stains. I want you to have something special this time; consider it my treat."

Hesitantly, Cara allowed James to buy her the white dress. As they exited the store, she said, "Thank you. I have to admit, having this dress makes me feel special."

"Good," James said with a smile. "That's what I want for you today."

When they arrived at the church, it was bustling with people moving around.

Cara turned to James with a puzzled look on her face. "What's going on? Why are so many people here?"

"Several of the townsfolk heard what happened and offered to help us with the wedding and reception," James explained.

Tears formed in the corner of her eyes; she was touched by the kind gesture from the townspeople. She never thought she would ever feel this happy again after her parents' death, but she had been wrong. A complete sense of belonging flooded her, making her grateful that she had finally found her place in the world. She belonged with the Cassidy family, and she would do whatever it took to keep them safe and happy as long as she had breath in her body.

Inside the church, hydrangeas lined the pews in pretty, white vases. There was also tulle draped between the pews, and candles lit around the area.

"This is beautiful," Cara said with awe. "I can't believe you planned all this."

"I had help," James admitted. "The town's women's auxiliary offered to set everything up for the wedding. They also mentioned they would love for you to join the organization once you're ready."

"I'd like that. I haven't felt like part of a community in a long time."

"Why don't you go get into your dress. Susan and Becky want to change with you since we bought them matching dresses for the occasion."

Cara and the girls made their way into the back room of the church. Susan helped Cara into her dress, fastening the long row of tiny buttons that ran up the back of it. Next, they fixed her hair, pinning it up but still allowing a few curls to fall down and wrap around Cara's neck.

James had insisted she get a veil too, so she

placed that at the top of her head, securing it with a couple of extra pins.

"You look beautiful," Susan said, tears forming in her eyes. "You might be the most beautiful bride I've ever seen."

"She is," Becky agreed. "Our Ma is perfect."

The girls got into their matching pale pink dresses with flowers embroidered along the sleeves and collar. Becky picked up a basket that had flower petals in it, excited to be able to scatter them for Cara's march down the aisle.

They exited out the back door of the church, Becky scampering ahead to make sure no one was lingering outside the church, while Susan carried the bottom of Cara's dress with one hand so it wouldn't get dirty.

At the top of the steps, Susan handed Cara her bouquet of white and pink flowers, while keeping a smaller version for herself.

"You ready, Ma?" Susan inquired with a smile. "This time, it's for keeps."

"I've never been more ready for anything in my life. I can't wait to officially become a Cassidy."

The piano from inside the church started to play music, signaling to the girls outside it was time to start the ceremony. The doors to the church opened. Susan gave Cara a quick hug, then headed down the aisle. Becky followed after, with her basket of flowers, blowing a kiss to Cara before she drifted off out of sight.

Cara was the last to head down the aisle. As her eyes settled on James standing in a striking dark brown suit, she realized she was heading towards the future she never imagined for herself, but one that was better than she could ever dream of. She was going to be Mrs. Cassidy, officially. A title she was proud to call her own.

———

As James watched Cara float down the aisle, his breath caught in his chest. She was the most breathtaking vision he had ever seen. Her red hair was artfully arranged on top of her head with a handful of curls cascading down and around her neck with her veil framing her face.

The dress he insisted she get was worth every penny he spent on it. It fit her perfectly, enhancing her slim frame and ample assets, making her the most gorgeous woman he had ever seen. He couldn't believe how blessed he was to have her agree to be his wife.

As Cara approached the front of the church, James reached out his hand to her. She placed hers in his, giving him an enchanting smile that made his heart skip a beat.

He leaned forward and whispered, "You look lovely."

"Thank you," she whispered back. "You look handsome too."

The pastor started to speak, welcoming the assembled guests, and talking about the commitments of marriage and love. James was aware the words were important and symbolic, but all he could do was focus on the beautiful woman standing next to him.

The marriage vows passed with ease, followed by the exchanging of the new rings James bought for Cara and him. He was grateful when the pastor asked them to simply slip them on each other's fingers and repeat their commitments to each other.

"Please turn and face your friends and family."

Cara and James did as the pastor asked.

"By the power vested in me by God, I now pronounce you, officially, husband and wife."

The crowd clapped and cheered as Cara and James turned to face each other.

"You may kiss your bride," the pastor added.

James leaned forward and placed his lips on Cara's, the connection in the moment so strong, James nearly thought he might pass out from the intoxicating effect.

They rushed down the aisle, ready to go to their reception and start their new lives together.

The reception was in the town square where the auxiliary had set up several tables for food and drinks as well as for guests to eat. There was also an area by the gazebo for the band to play later for dancing.

The children rushed up and begged them to eat with them. Cara and James obliged, letting them lead them to a table at the front of the square. The auxiliary planned a potluck, and everyone had brought their favorite dishes to share. James enjoyed the food, but nothing was as good as when Cara cooked for him.

After the meal concluded, James and Cara spent a bit of time greeting all their guests before it was time for the cake cutting. Once they shared the first piece of the layered vanilla baked goodness, it was time for the first dance.

James took Cara up the stairs that led to the gazebo, then gathered her into his arms in the center of it. The music started to play and they both swayed to the music.

"I can't believe how lucky we are to find one another," Cara gushed. "I'm happier than I ever thought I could be."

"We're not just lucky, we're blessed because God guided us to each other. I never knew I could love again after Laura, but my heart is fuller now than I ever thought possible. You're the best thing to ever happen to me, Cara, and I love you so much my heart is about to burst out of my chest because of how full you've made it."

Cara leaned up and kissed her husband on the lips. "I love you too, I can't wait to spend the rest of my life with you."

The children rushed up and joined them on the dance floor. Thomas tapped his father on the shoulder and demanded, "I think it's time for me to dance with my Ma now."

James chuckled, then stepped back. "Why, of course, young sir, enjoy." From the edge of the gazebo, James watched as his son awkwardly placed his hand on Cara's waist, then used his other hand to take one of hers. Though he was half as tall as her, it was precious to see how serious he took the dance.

"Would you like to dance, Pa?" Susan asked, her cheeks tinged pink from all the excitement of the night.

"I'd love to, Susan," he said with a grin, walking with her to dance next to Cara and Thomas.

"You know, I was wrong about her, Pa. Cara is the perfect person to be our new mother. No one will ever replace our first ma, but Cara is exactly what we need now. I'm so glad she's part of our family now."

"I agree. She's just what we need."

A couple songs later, James was finally able to grab his bride for another dance.

"It feels like forever since I held you in my arms," James lamented with a tiny frown. "It seems now that you're mine, I don't want to share you with anyone else."

"You won't ever have to, James. I'm yours, mind, body and soul, forever." Almost as if on cue, Becky and Thomas rushed up and pushed their way in between them. Then with a wink, she added, "Well, there are three others that I belong to as well."

"I'm okay with that," James said with a chuckle. "It's how it's supposed to be."

———

Want to find out more about Riker? Check out the next book in the series, <u>Mail Order Misstep</u>, where he makes another appearance.

SNEAK PEAK OF MAIL ORDER MISSTEP

Laurel, Mississippi 1885

"Listen here, girl, you'll do what I say," Elsie Jenkins' papa bellowed at her in a thick Southern accent, his round face bright red as the veins around his beady, brown eyes, and his thick neck bulged with rage. "I've put a roof over your head and food in your belly for nearly two decades now, and your marryin' Arthur Dorin is finally gonna put a little money back in my pocket."

"Papa, you can't mean to make me do it." Elsie pleaded as she pulled on the sleeve of her father's dingy cream shirt. "Mr. Dorin is an awful man. He beat his first wife before she died from consumption."

"Then you should learn from her mistakes, Elsie, and be a compliant wife. If you do what your husband says, he won't have a need to beat you." Her father yanked free and raised his fist in the air. "As it is, you're testin' my own patience with your whinin'. I have a good mind to show you what a sound beating is."

Elsie dropped her hand to her side and stumbled backward until she was flush against the rough wall of their small farmhouse, causing her red locks to bounce around her face. Shocked and frightened by his threat, she wrapped her arms around herself as if they were a shield. Her papa couldn't be described as a kind man, but neither had he ever proven to be a violent one. At least, she hadn't thought him to be, until she saw the menacing look in his eyes as he stomped towards her.

Her papa slammed his fist into the wall beside her face, causing her to flinch and look away. "You'll marry Arthur Dorin by week's end, or you'll be turned out from my home quicker than you can blink an eye. Do I make myself clear, Elsie?"

"Yes, Papa," she whispered, in her own soft

Southern accent, as tears filled the corners of her green eyes. "I understand."

"Good, that's a good girl." Her papa moved his hand over from the wall and patted the top of her head. "You don't need to show any of that stubbornness you got from your mother. By golly, it was the bane of my blight. I don't need you goin' and thinkin' you can act like her."

What Elsie wouldn't give for her mama to still be alive. Her Irish pride would've never stood for Elsie's papa selling Elsie off like a prized-cow. Her mama would've protected Elsie at all costs. But life wasn't fair, and Elsie had been without her mama for the past five years after she died in childbirth, along with her baby sister. Elsie had been left with only her selfish papa to take care of her. He demanded Elsie work her fingers to the bone and gave her little more than a passing thought until Arthur Dorin came sniffing around. She hadn't thought her situation could get any worse, but when Mr. Dorin offered to pay her father a windfall of money for her, she knew any chance at having a happy life was over.

"Now, go on and make supper before I change my mind about that beating."

Elsie scurried off towards the kitchen, pulling

out the items she needed to turn last night's dinner into a stew. She set to work filling the pot with water and placing it on the stove before cutting up the vegetables. Her hands continued on the task as her mind raced with thoughts of what she could do to escape Arthur Dorin's clutches.

She could tell from her father's resolve, it didn't matter how good she treated him or how hard she worked around the farm, he wanted the money more than he wanted her help. That meant she had to find another way out of the horrible situation.

Could she ask someone at the church for help? No, their pastor would tell her that it was her duty to obey her father. What about someone in town? Could she find a place to stay and work if her father kicked her out like he promised? No, they wouldn't want to get involved. What else could she do? Runaway? If she did, where would she go? How would she provide for herself? She doubted there were very many reputable options for a young woman, but it only took one. Tomorrow when she was in town picking up supplies, she would look through the newspaper. Silently, she sent up a prayer asking God to help her find a way out of the mess her papa put her in.

"How are you doing today, Miss Elsie?" Bonnie Trivail asked as Elsie entered the mercantile. "Are you here to pick up your weekly supplies?"

Elsie nodded. "Thank you, Miss Bonnie. I'd also like a copy of the newspaper."

The older brunette woman raised her eyebrows at the unusual request but handed one over without comment. Elsie collected the rest of her supplies, then hurried out of the store to the nearest bench. She didn't have long before her papa would become suspicious of her absence, and she would need every minute to form a plan of escape.

Elsie flipped open the paper to the 'help wanted' area. She skimmed through it, and just as she suspected, there wasn't a single job that a God-fearing woman would consider. What was she going to do? She couldn't stay in Laurel and marry Mr. Dorin, but what other choice did she have?

"What are you doing here, sitting all by yourself, Elsie?"

She glanced up and was relieved to see Sarah Johnson, her good friend from school. "I was just looking through the newspaper before I headed home."

"Why would you need to read anything in there?" Sarah inquired, her face scrunching up with disdain. "It's just gobs of bad news and dubious requests from strangers."

"Have you heard what my papa wants me to do?"

"Of course I have. Everyone else in town has too. I'm sorry that he's forcing you to marry Mr. Dorin." Sarah took a seat next to her friend on the bench. "I know you'd hoped for a better life than that."

"It's not that I don't want to get married. If it was to a kind and gentle man, I wouldn't object. Mr. Dorin, however, is a shrewd scoundrel. Who knew my father would turn me over to him for the right amount of money?"

"It doesn't seem fair that our lives are decided by the men in them, does it?" Sarah lamented. "My own father has decided that I'm to marry his business partner's son."

"At least Roger is a good man and will treat you fairly," Elsie pointed out. "Though I know you had your heart set on Lucas."

Lucas was the pastor's son and had attended school with all of them. He didn't have much in the way of means, which meant that Sarah's father didn't find him a suitable match for his daughter.

Sarah pressed her lips together as she squeezed her hands in her lap and shrugged with resignation. "What choice do we have?"

"I can't accept that being Mr. Dorin's second wife will be my future. There has to be something I can do about it."

"Besides running away and becoming a mail-order bride," Sarah teased with a giggle, "I don't see what choice you have."

"A mail-order bride," Elsie repeated. "Now, that isn't a bad idea."

"I wasn't serious, Elsie," Sarah rebuked. "You know those things are a scam, and half the time you arrive to find your groom is as ugly as a toad and twice as mean. You're better off with the devil you know, than agreeing to such a thing."

"You're wrong, Sarah. Sometimes those marriages do work out. My cousin has a loving, kind husband out West. She found him through an advert in the…" Elsie snapped her fingers as she recalled the name, *Matrimonial Times*—that's the name of the newspaper where the men place their requests." Glancing over at her friend, she requested in a hopeful tone, "Do you mind going into the mercantile and grabbing me a copy so my papa doesn't find out?"

Sarah's eyes grew round with bewilderment. "You can't be serious, Elsie. I don't want my own father thinking I'm planning on jilting my fiancé. You're going to have to find someone else to do your dirty work."

Out of the corner of her eye, Elsie noticed ten-year-old Billy Thudrow playing with a can and stick on the other side of Main Street. "Billy, do you mind coming over here for a minute? I need to ask you to do me a favor."

Billy scampered across the street, curiosity filling his eyes. "What kind of favor?"

"I need you to go into the mercantile and buy something for me."

"What do I get out of it?" he asked, as his eyes narrowed slightly in a calculating way.

"How about I give you enough to get a penny candy?"

"How about three?" Billy countered as he pushed out his hand with three fingers sticking straight up in the air.

"Two, and I won't tell your mama you pulled Linda's hair at church last Sunday," Elsie threatened with a sly smile.

Billy's eyebrows shot up in fright as he quickly nodded his head. "Two is fine. What you need me to buy for you, Miss Elsie?"

"It's a newspaper called the Matrimonial Times. It's right on the counter." Elsie handed over the money and waited as the boy scampered off to retrieve the requested item.

A few minutes later, he returned with the newspaper in his hands. He was sucking on a candy as he shoved the sheets of paper towards Elsie. "I told Miss Bonnie it was for my cousin who's stayin' with us. I figured you didn't want her to know it was for you."

"Thank you, Billy," Elsie said with a smile. She didn't like the fact the boy lied to cover up her deeds, but it did make it easier for her to keep her plans from her papa.

Elsie scanned the adverts, hope rising in her that maybe she didn't have to marry Mr. Dorin after all. "Let's see what other options are out there."

"I can't believe you're doing this, Elsie." Sarah shook her head, crossing her arms over her chest. "To be willing to leave Laurel to go out West to marry a complete stranger seems like such a wild and reckless idea."

"I'm desperate, Sarah. Mr. Dorin is not an

acceptable option, and my papa has left me with no other choice."

The first few men who placed adverts were not to her liking. They either were too old or requested odd qualifications, but the fifth one stopped her quick enough. She read it over and over. By the third time through it, she realized she might have found her way out from the rotten future her father had planned for her.

In immediate need of a strong, independent, young woman open to marrying a Pinkerton agent, requiring a steadfast, devoted wife. Must be willing to travel wherever the job demands, and keep the fire burning while away on assignments. Only a serious miss need apply via telegraph.

The wife of a Pinkerton agent? Could she agree to such a thing? She fit all of the man's requirements, and she could maintain a home the way he needed. "I have to go, Sarah. I'll talk to you later."

Elsie rushed across the street to the telegraph office. She pulled out the little bit of money she'd been secretly saving out of the supply money each week. Once she determined how much she could afford, she responded.

Resilient and capable at 19, ready to provide a refuge in the form of a home and commit to an agent in need.

"I'll check back tomorrow for an answer," Elsie explained to the telegraph operator. "I'd appreciate your discretion."

Luckily, the postmaster wasn't a fan of her papa after he sold his wife some chickens no longer capable of laying eggs. Elsie was rather certain he wouldn't go out of his way to tell him about her correspondence with the man out West.

When she returned home, she purposely hid one of the items to give herself an excuse to head back into town the following day. Hopefully, she would find the answer she needed to escape out West and leave her father and his despicable plans for her far behind.

Grab your copy of Mail Order Misstep.

ALSO BY JENNA BRANDT

Most Books are Free in Kindle Unlimited too!

Mail Order Mix-Up Series-mail order bride books about women venturing out West to make new lives for themselves. What happens when they decide to take a chance on love along the way?

Mail Order Misfit

Mail Order Misstep

Mail Order Miscast

Mail Order Misaim

Mail Order Misplay

Mail Order Mister

Mail Order Mishap

Widows, Brides, and Secret Babies-mail order bride stories with a twist. What happens when a bride arrives pregnant or with a secret child?

Mail Order Miranda

Mail Order Miriam

Secret Baby Dilemma-each mail order bride arrives with a baby or pregnant, and the prospective groom doesn't know until her arrival.

Mail Order Madeline

The Civil War Brides Trilogy-during the bloodiest conflict on American soil, two families struggle in the South to not only survive but to thrive.

Saved by Faith

Freed by Hope

Healed by Grace

Border Brides Series-centered around the Old West border towns and the brides who end up there looking for a new start.

Discreetly Matched

June's Remedy

Becca's Lost Love

Hard to Please

The Window to the Heart Saga is a recountal of the epic journey of Lady Margaret, a young English noblewoman, who through many trials, obstacles, and tragedies, discovers her own inner strength, the sustaining force of faith in God, and the power of family and friends. In this three-part series, experience new places and cultures as the heroine travels from England to France and completes her adventures in America. The series has compelling themes of love, loss, faith and hope with an exceptionally gratifying conclusion.

Trilogy

The English Proposal (Book 1)

The French Encounter (Book 2)

The American Conquest (Book 3)

Spin-offs

The Oregon Pursuit (Book 1)

The White Weddings (Book 2)

The Viscount's Wife (Book 3)

The Window to the Heart Saga
Trilogy Box Set

The Window to the Heart Saga
Spin-off Books Box Set

The Window to the Heart Saga

Complete Collection Box Set

The Lawkeepers is a multi-author series alternating between historical westerns and contemporary westerns featuring law enforcement heroes that span multiple agencies and generations. Join bestselling author Jenna Brandt and many others as they weave captivating, sweet and inspirational stories of romance and suspense between the lawkeepers — and the women who love them. The Lawkeepers is a world like no other; a world where lawkeepers and heroes are honored with unforgettable stories, characters, and love. Jenna's Lawkeeper books:

Historical

Lawfully Loved-Texas Sheriff

Lawfully Wanted-Bounty Hunter

Lawfully Forgiven-Texas Ranger

Lawfully Avenged-US Marshal

Lawfully Covert-Spies

Lawfully Historical Box Set

Contemporary

Lawfully Adored-K-9

Lawfully Wedded-K-9

Disaster City Search and Rescue

Step into the world of Disaster City Search and Rescue, where officers, firefighters, military, and medics, train and work alongside each other with the dogs they love, to do the most dangerous job of all — help lost and injured victims find their way home.

The Boss's Baby Rescue

Wild Animal Protection Agency

Come be apart of the adventure, danger, and heartfelt moments with the Wild Animal Protection Agency, where brave men and women work alongside each other all over the world, to do the most risky job of all — rescue injured and endangered wild animals.

Rescue Agent for Dana

Rescue Agent for Sarah

Rescue Agent for Kylie

Rescue Agent for Josette

Rescue Agent for Margo

Rescue Agent for Penny

Billionaire Birthday Club is an exclusive resort—for the billionaire who appears to have everything but secretly wants more. After filling out a confidential survey, a curated celebration is waiting on the island to make their birthday wishes come true!

The Billionaire's Birthday Wish

The Billionaire's Birthday Surprise

The Billionaire's Birthday Gift

Billionaires of Manhattan Series

The billionaires that live in Manhattan and the women who love them. If you love epic dates, grand romantic gestures, and men in suits with hearts of gold, then these are books are perfect for you.

Waiting on the Billionaire

Nanny for the Billionaire

Merging with the Billionaire

(Entire series on Audiobook)

Second Chance Islands-What's better than billionaires on islands? How about billionaires finding second chances at life, love, and redemption while on one.

The Billionaire's Repeat

(Free the you join my newsletter)

The Billionaire's Reunion

The Billionaire's Hideaway

The Billionaire's Duty

The Billionaire's Christmas

For more information about Jenna Brandt, signup for her Newsletter or visit her on any of her social media platforms:

www.JennaBrandt.com

www.facebook.com/JennaBrandtAuthor

Jenna Brandt's Reader Group

www.twitter.com/JennaDBrandt

www.instagram.com/jennabrandtauthor

ACKNOWLEDGMENTS

My writing journey would not be possible without those who supported me. Since I can remember, writing is the only thing I love to do, and my deepest desire is to share my talent with others.

First and foremost, I am eternally grateful to Jesus, my lord and savior, who created me with this "writing bug" DNA.

In addition, many thanks go to:

My husband, Dustin, and three daughters, Katie, Julie, and Nikki, for loving me and supporting me during all my late-night writing marathons and coffee-infused mornings.

My mother, Connie, for being my first and most honest critic. As a little girl, sleeping under your desk during late-night deadlines for the local paper showed me what being a dedicated writer looked like.

My angels in heaven: my grandmother, who passed away in 2001; my infant son, Dylan, who was taken by SIDS seven years ago; and my father, who left us six years ago.

To Ginny Sterling and Jo Grafford, my best writing buddies, my comrades-in-arms, my sounding boards, my voices of reason, my partners in all things author. I love you ladies so much.

To my ARC Angels and Beta Bells for taking the time to read my story and give valuable feedback.

And lastly, but so important, to my dedicated readers, who have shared their love of my books with others, helping to spread the words about my stories. Your devotion means a great deal.

ABOUT THE AUTHOR

Jenna Brandt is an international bestselling and award-winning author who writes historical and contemporary romance. Her historical books span from Victorian to Western eras and all of her books have elements of romance, suspense and faith. She has her own best-selling historical series, Window to the Heart Saga, Mail Order Mix-Up, and Civil War Brides, as well as contemporary series, Billionaires of Manhattan, Second Chance Islands and the Wild Animal Protection Agency. Additionally, she's created two best-selling multi-author series, The Lawkeepers and Disaster City Search and Rescue based off the life of her husband in law enforcement. Both of her books, Waiting on the Billionaire and Lawfully Treasured, were voted into the Top 50 Indie Books of 2018 and her book, The Billionaire's Birthday Gift, was a finalist in the "Best Book We've Read All Year" Contest in 2020.

She's been an avid reader since she could hold a book and started writing stories almost as early. She's been published in several newspapers as well as edited for multiple papers, and graduated with her Bachelor of Arts degree in English from Bethany College where she was the Editor-in-Chief of the newspaper. Her first blog was published on The Mighty website, Yahoo Parenting and The Grief Toolbox as well as featured on the ABC News, CNN Health, and Good Morning America websites. She's also a member of the American Christian Fiction Writers (ACFW) association.

Writing is her passion, but she also enjoys date nights with her hubby, cooking from scratch, watching movies on Netflix, reading books by her author friends, and engaging in social media with her readers. Her three young daughters keep her busy with Girl Scout activities, going to the mall, and playing at the park where they live in the Central Valley of California. She summers on the Golden Central Coast where she finds endless inspiration for her romance books. She's also active in her local church where she volunteers on their first impressions team.